W9-ADJ-204

DISCARD
No longer property
of the Pierson Library

House *of* Dance

Also by Beth Kephart:

UNDERCOVER

House *of* Dance

BETH KEPHART

LAURA GERINGER BOOKS
HARPER TEEN
An Imprint of HarperCollins*Publishers*

HarperTeen is an imprint of HarperCollins Publishers.

House of Dance
Copyright © 2008 by Beth Kephart
All rights reserved. Printed in the United States of America.
No part of this book may be used or reproduced in any manner whatsoever
without written permission except in the case of brief quotations embodied
in critical articles and reviews. For information address
HarperCollins Children's Books, a division of HarperCollins Publishers,
1350 Avenue of the Americas, New York, NY 10019.
www.harperteen.com

Library of Congress Cataloging-in-Publication Data
Kephart, Beth.
House of Dance / by Beth Kephart. — 1st ed.
    p.   cm.
"HarperTeen."
Summary: During one of her daily visits across town to visit her dying
grandfather, fifteen-year-old Rosie discovers a dance studio that helps her find
a way to give her grandfather one last gift.
ISBN 978-0-06-142928-6 (trade bdg.) — ISBN 978-0-06-142929-3 (lib. bdg.)
[1. Grandfathers—Fiction. 2. Cancer—Fiction. 3. Ballroom dancing—Fiction.
4. Mothers and daughters—Fiction.] I. Title.
PZ7.K438Ho 2008   2007026011
[Fic]—dc22   CIP
                                                                      AC

Typography by Larissa Lawrynenko
1 2 3 4 5 6 7 8 9 10

First Edition

For my father,
who took such good care

ONE

IN THE SUMMER my mother grew zinnias in her window boxes and let fireflies hum through our back door. She kept basil alive in ruby-colored glasses and potatoes sprouting tentacles on the sills. On her bedroom ceiling she'd pressed glow-in-the-dark dots into constellation patterns, so that the stars, as she put it, would always be near. Andromeda. Aquarius. The major and minor Ursas. Pisces. Creatures with wings or with horns.

When I was younger, I'd lie beside her, with all those stars pressing in like tattoos. I'd listen for the wind through the trees, or a finch with a song, or music from the Burkeman house next door. "Not a word, Rosie," she would say. "Let the day be," and my thoughts would float until they drifted toward something that was fixed and sure. My mother cleaned windows for Mr. Paul. She spent her days looking through other people's worlds. In her own house, she said, she needed quiet to remember who she was.

"Not a word, Rosie. Not a single one." You could get a lot of thinking done when you were with my mother. You could ask yourself a million questions.

I was nine and ten and eleven and twelve. My dad, who had left us years before for what he called a scratchy itch, had never made it home. He sent me twenty dollars every week. Proof, he wrote in his notebook-paper scribbles, that he loved me still. I kept the cash in a shoe box in the bottom of my closet, behind a crate of used-up toys. Proof, I'd have said, if he had asked me, that love cannot be bought.

I was thirteen, I was fourteen, I was fifteen. My mother still cleaned windows, still left the house every day in her stained overalls, her cantaloupe-colored rubber gloves, her denim visor. Except that now she and Mr. Paul were what she called partners, and her days were that much longer, and there were no more potatoes with octopus tentacles on the sill. Sometimes Mom didn't get home until midnight. Sometimes she was, in the softest voice, singing. Sometimes she forgot that I was there at all, and that is why what happened happened. Because I had been put in charge of myself, and my grandfather was dying.

He didn't live far; he never had. He'd always been where he was, on the other side of the train tracks, on the opposite end of town, at the final step of a twenty-minute walk. You'd go down to the end of my street. You'd turn.

You'd walk beneath the big stone railroad bridge, where there was wetness no matter what the temperature was, something like stalactites daggering down. You'd get back out into the windswept air and go up the hill and turn left onto the street of shops: Whiz Bang, the balloons and party favors store; the deli named Pastrami's; Sweet Loaves Bread; Mr. Harvey's Once-Read Books; Bloomer's Flowers; the hardware store that had become a discount drugstore that was now a sort of everything store, where the mannequins never changed the clothes they wore and the same rocking chair kept rocking.

It was all redbrick on either side, and above the ground-floor retail there were second-story rooms where people I never did see lived, hung their birdcages on curtain rods and umbrellas out their windows, left their happy birthday signs and colored streamers for months and months on end.

My grandfather lived at the edge of all

that, in a house of six rooms and one attic, the first house past retail, he called it. When I was little, he would sit in a chair on his porch all summer, watching the cars and the bikes and the buses go by, reading his *National Geographic* magazines and expedition catalogs. My grandmother had died before I was born. I'd known him only as a man who said there had been places he might have gone, regrets that he'd got stuck with, times that had slipped away like sand. I'd known him only as my mother's father until the summer he got sick. "Rosie," my mom said, the night she told me, "he's going to need you now."

"What do you want me to do?"

"What you can, Rosie. Whatever you can."

My mother had long, dark hair. It was her shield, her protection. She turned her face and I couldn't see her eyes, and I could not for the life of me guess what it was she planned to do. "How sick, Mom?" I asked.

"Multiple myeloma, Rosie."

"What does that mean?"

She sighed, and it was a very sad sound. She looked away from me. "That he's tired. That he'd like to see you. That I need you to help him through this. Help me."

My mother was an only child like I was an only child. I stared at her black, silky profile. "I bet he'd like to see you, too," I said.

"*Rosie*," she said.

And I was quiet. Because of course I knew that they had had their falling-out, that they hadn't been speaking, not lately. Of course I knew. Still, he was dying. Still, she was letting their argument, or whatever it was, be bigger than the love she felt inside. That was how I saw it anyway.

Truth of it was that school had let out two weeks before, and I was still angling for a purpose. My best friend, Leisha, had gone off to the shore to play nanny to her cousins, who were three, four, and five and hot spikes of trouble. Nick Burkeman from next door was working at his father's shop, lying under cars all day and staring at their bellies, even though what he loved most was the great outdoors, something his father called useless. Everyone else I knew had gotten some kind of gainful employment—at the pool or the mall or the movie theater—or was prepping for the SATs with a tutor who came to breakfast. "Your tutor eats breakfast at your house?" I'd said to Rocco, in May, in disbelief. "Yeah," Rocco had answered, rolling his eyes. "Yeah. That's right. He does. Barks vocab words at me when I'm buttering my toast."

Before Granddad got sick, my mom had said that I could work with her and Mr. Paul, six dollars an hour, two mornings a week, the summer season. But their happiness together was the kind that made you feel banned, barred, and excluded, and besides, I couldn't imagine cleaning other people's windows, whisking things off their windowsills, altering the color of their sun. Besides all that, Mom didn't mean it. She wanted, it was so obvious, to be alone with Mr. Paul and the sheets of glass. She had earned, she made it clear, that little smudge of joy. It didn't matter to Mom that Mr. Paul was married. She'd been taken from, that was her thinking, and now it was her turn for taking.

My granddad was the kind of person you had to look for to find. He'd be in a room and you'd know it, but you'd have to think real hard to remember. He'd be across from you at the kitchen table, and you'd forget to offer him the salt. Granddad said that he preferred to listen, and it was as if he'd been God-engineered for that, his eyes big, blue, and round, his ears overlarge and tipped forward, his body short and wiry as an antenna. He had the most beautiful white hair I'd ever seen and hands that he held still upon his lap. He wore dark sweaters in the winter with khaki-colored pants and black socks, and in the summer he wore the very same pants and white, short-sleeved shirts, but no socks. He called these things his traveling duds, as if he were going somewhere. Patagonia, he'd say. The Sea of Cortés. Bhutan. The places in his dog-eared magazines.

The first day of that long summer changed everything for good. It was the end of June but not yet hot, the sky filled up with so many kinds of clouds, with blue behind the clouds, not gray. There was a breeze. Granddad had left his screen door unlatched, and so I went straight on through, out of the breeze and into his skinny yellow kitchen. Right there on the counter, first thing, were a swamp of bowls and a rusty can opener, a pileup of dish towels and a couple of old, rain-spotted magazines. The kitchen needed straightening up.

"Granddad?" I called. "Grand . . . dad?" I let the screen door close behind me and began walking down the long rubber runner on the linoleum kitchen floor and through to his dining room, which was also his living room, where almost every inch of wall was lined with shelves, and the shelves were not nearly enough. There were books on the floor beside newspapers, old coffee cups in stacks in corners, a couple of tossed-aside spoons, a crooked pile of baskets beside a TV that didn't look capable of pictures or sound, the parts of something alongside the couch that, it suddenly occurred to me, were the pieces of the sort of record player I'd seen once in a movie. The only place the walls weren't plastered over with shelves was this one long closet—floor to ceiling with two heavy paneled doors. I'd never seen that closet open. I didn't want to think about what was inside.

Besides the dining-room table and its four mismatched chairs, there were two stuffed corduroy La-Z-Boys and a couch, brown cow–colored, and on the coffee table, which was low to the ground, there was a wicker basket from which Riot, Granddad's Maine coon cat, ruled. She had the longest tail I'd ever seen on a cat and pointy espionage ears, and she was all possession, guarding Granddad, who was asleep on the couch. He'd folded one arm under his head, and his long, bare feet, thin, like my mother's, but also callused, were twitching. His eyelids were rolled partway down over his eyes, and there was the tent of a magazine staked up on his stomach, the Trans-Siberian something. I sat down on a La-Z-Boy. Riot hissed and showed her fangs. She tried to stare me down. I waited for something to happen. I thought maybe the walls would come tumbling down.

"Did you see your grandfather today?" Mom asked me hours later, calling into my bedroom through the dark.

"Yeah," I said. And that was all I said. I didn't say that he hadn't seen me.

The next day I didn't get up until sometime

after ten, long after my mother had left. I toasted my bread and I poured my juice and I washed the plate and the glass. Through the kitchen window I could see Mrs. Robertson hanging her sheets on the line, and her short white slips. I'd grown up knowing that square was the shape of all her underwear. That she gave Butterfingers for Halloween. That she'd lost her only son and her daughter was long gone. That she kept one light on in her basement always, grew monster-size tomatoes, and had a cat named Claw that had a single working eye, a scruffy tail, a belly so big we all called him fat as a statement of fact and not as some grand insult.

But mostly Mrs. Robertson was a mystery, and that was my thought of the hour: that maybe all of us are. That Granddad had been young before he'd been old. That Mom had been a daughter once, like me. That there were things on the verge of vanishing that I barely understood.

TWO

B Y THE TIME I set off for the opposite end
of town, the air in the railroad tunnel
was all green steam, and there was a loose
dog toddling about with his tongue rolled
out, taking a frothy stroll. Sweet Loaves had
propped open its front door with a stool, and
where the green steam ended there was the
smell of cinnamon sugar and risen dough,
sesame seeds sizzled by an oven. It was past
noon. A neon balloon had escaped Whiz
Bang, and when I looked up to watch it on its
way to nowhere, my ears caught the end of

another country's song. It had come from somewhere second story, and I waited, but there was no more. I waited; then I walked on. Stopped to study the window at Harvey's Once Read, where Harvey had, as he always did, posted the week's doggerel. He wrote up a new one every Monday, and each was as bad as the last, but he didn't know it. Harvey loved authors and Harvey loved himself, and you couldn't step inside his shop without saying some version of "I'm loving the new doggerel."

At Pastrami's you didn't have to pretend. At Pastrami's everything—big hanks of pink meat, sweating wedges of cheese, wide tumbles of tomatoes—was piled high, and down low, in front of the big backward-sloping cases, were the barrels of pickles that Mom once said had been floating on their backs forever. Mr. D'Imperio was a very large size. His eyes behind his glasses were three times magnified, so out of proportion to his face that once when I saw him in the street without his glasses on, I didn't know who he was until I heard "Rosie" the way he says "Rosie," with the longest O you ever heard, as if I were his favorite niece. Mr. D'Imperio made his sandwiches with a mustard so bittersweet that it was enough, sometimes, just to have a slab of black bread with a mustard spread, which he gave out for free, at least to me, when nobody was watching. That day I leaned into the door and the door chimes chimed. I took a number and waited my turn. I watched the pickles floating.

"I hope you like turkey," I called out when I pushed through Granddad's door.

"Rosie?" His voice was dim and far away. "Is that you?"

"Special delivery from Pastrami's," I said, trailing through and finding him where I'd left him the day before, the same pair of pants on, the same bare toes, the Trans-Siberian something flipped upright on his lap. I pulled his sandwich and pickle out of a bag. I pulled the same out for me. Riot gave me her I-do-not-trust-you eye, then settled back in for a snooze.

"How are you doing, Granddad?" I asked.

"I had this dream," he said, after a long, quiet time.

"What kind of dream?"

"Somewhere far away. Somewhere. And they were playing music."

"Might not have been a dream," I suggested, and I was about to say that I had heard something too, but he preferred his own conclusion.

"Oh, yes." He was sure. "It was." He struggled up, to a sitting position. He unwrapped the turkey sandwich. He looked at me. Studied the sandwich and raised it to his mouth but didn't so much as taste it. "To what do I owe this pleasure, Miss Rosie?" finally he asked me.

"I needed some company," I said, chomping at my own lunch, feeling around with my tongue for the mustard. Wishing he would chomp on his, because he was pants-loose thin.

"You did." He eyed me suspiciously.

I swallowed. "It gets lonely in my house."

"Where's your mother?"

"Cleaning windows."

He brought the sandwich to his mouth again, then lowered it onto his Trans-Siberian journey, untested. He looked around as if to study the state of his own windows, which, truth be told, were streaked with old rain and whitened, in certain places, by spiderwebs; he could have used some Mr. Paul. "Can't say as there's a lot of action here."

"You're here," I said. "And so is Riot."

"Riot"—Granddad nodded—"doesn't stop talking." He looked at the basket, where Riot was sleeping. Then he looked at me. "How have you been, Rosie?"

17

"Same as always," I said.

"How old are you now?"

"Fifteen."

"School out?"

"Until it starts again."

"Did you ride your bike?"

"I walked."

"You walked?"

And then we both sat while I ate in silence.

THREE

I DIDN'T LEAVE GRANDDAD'S until the moon was brighter than the sun. Along the redbrick strip the doors to first-floor shops were closed, the bargain tables dragged in for the night, the books at Mr. Harvey's a little more faded than before. Any light and noise came from the floors above: the sizzle of hamburgers in a frying pan, the sound of TV news, the slamming of doors, someone fighting with a stubborn window. A dog was barking, and I remembered the afternoon's mongrel. But mostly I was looking for the music that I'd heard, keeping my eyes on the second stories.

It was when I reached the intersection and turned right, toward the railroad tunnel, that I saw something I had never had reason before to look up and see: a row of large, lit-up windows, all of them belonging to one room, and not one of them curtained over. Beyond the windows there were mirrors, and between the windows and the mirrors there was dance. A girl frowning at her own reflection. A man with jet black hair dancing beside her, explaining something, placing his hands on her hips, swirling her body. A couple out on the edge of things, strung up, it seemed, by puppet strings. Someone had pushed open the wood-frame windows, and through the windows music drifted. Another country's music.

I stood in the shadows of the Sweet Loaves awning and leaned against its door. I watched the arms and the heads and the whirl of dancers, the man with the black hair demonstrating. The couple cut a diagonal across the room. The girl in front of the mirror swirled her hips in a figure eight, and then the black-haired man ironed her shoulders flat and talked until she shook her head the wrong way, saying no to something—so much no that she proved it now by stomping away even as he stood where he was, still talking. Passersby just walked on past, not seeing. Every once in a while a train went rumbling by on the tracks, and the dog would bark, and the cars would brake and accelerate again. Someone in the room above Sweet Loaves snapped on a TV show and coughed.

Nobody anywhere was waiting for me. I could watch for as long as I wanted, and I did, because now the girl had come back to the black-haired guy's talking, and now they were a yes, a one thing moving; they were a tree that branched apart above their joined-together legs and hips. They danced, and he stopped her. He held her still and rearranged

21

her chin, pushed her face away from his, and up, and then they moved again, together. The music was gone, and they didn't care. They were dancing again, so together and so apart. They were all lit up in their box of windows. I was there, and they didn't know it, and if they had, they wouldn't have cared.

FOUR

"HOW OLD," I asked Granddad the next day, "is Riot?"

"About your age."

"And what can she do besides sleep?"

"Preen."

"A purposeful life," I said.

"Aren't guests," he asked, "supposed to be polite?" I had bought yesterday's cinnamon buns at Sweet Loaves for half the price. I was eating mine with a fork, like cake, counting the raisins and wishing Granddad would eat. "You must be worth a fortune," he'd said when I'd pulled the buns from the bag. "First turkey sandwiches, now this."

"A trust fund babe," I'd said.

Now we were quiet. I'd found him upright when I'd stepped in, sitting in a chair, not reclining on the couch. He'd been reading one of those getaway magazines. He'd put it down, removed his glasses, and looked me up and down, shoulder to shoulder, as if I had changed since yesterday, become someone new.

"So," he said, after a bunch of motor-cyclists had gunned at the corner light and startled all three of us out of the messy silence, "I had an idea."

"What's that?" I pulled one more raisin out of the sweet, fat bread and placed my plate on the table.

"I need someone to help me get things straight around here."

I looked at the spill of it all, the triple-stacked books, the old newspapers, the stacks of paper cups, last night's dishes. The spiderweb in the nearest window was white and thick as Santa's beard. The candlesticks on the mantel were burned down to squat nubs. There were photographs in piles, like used-up decks of cards. There were Tupperware containers inside containers, preserving empty space. "Well, that's a surprise," I said.

"I'm willing to pay."

"Mom's the one with the clean touch," I said.

"Your mom's not here."

I looked around again at all his stuff. I looked more closely at him. At his thick white hair and pale white skin. At his eyes— more blue, more round than ever. At his feet, so long and thin. At his satellite dishes for ears. "I don't want your money, Granddad. You're going to need it."

"What could I need money for?"

"For doctors. For hospitals."

"I've had my fill."

"Mom says it's in your bones."

"Enough," he said. "Okay?" Riot was yawning and arching and kneading at the orange pillow in her wicker basket. She settled back in for a new nap.

"Riot's a funny name for your cat," I said into the silence.

"Life is awfully ironic."

I thought about Leisha at the shore with her crazy cousins—Leisha, who couldn't keep a notebook organized or her own room straight, but who was so glamorously, enviably, fabulously tall that the world at large could never guess at her disorder. I thought about Nick, messing with the innards of those cars when what he loved was sky. I thought about Mom and how all she said she wanted in life was quiet, and how all she had been doing lately was tempting big-time trouble. I thought about me and the summer ahead and how I'd been angling for a purpose. "What kind of keeping straight were you thinking of?" I asked at last.

"I want to put my things in order."

"Where were you thinking of starting?"

"Down here." He glanced around the room, toward the bookshelves.

"Do you have a thing for old newspapers?" I asked.

"No, I don't, Rosie. Not anymore."

"Do you have some string?"

"I think there is some in the kitchen."

"Does that record player work?" I asked.

"We could find out," he said, "some other day."

"Then let's find out. Okay?"

"There'll be plenty of time for that."

Sure, I thought. *Right*. But I was silent.

Riot shook her head and yawned and stretched again. She took a sudden leap off the table, her long tail swooshing the air. She put herself on parade about the room, shook out the mane on her bobcatish head.

"We have disturbed the queen," I said.

"Rosie Keith," Granddad said, "you talk

27

about your friends that way?"

"No," I said. Then: "Sometimes."

"You still friends with that boy next door?"

I felt my face go hot. I didn't answer.

"Nick," he said. "Nick B—something. Do I have that right?" He looked at me, made a funny Santa Claus smile. I shook my head, still not answering. Some things are private.

"So where do you hide your string?" I said.

"It'll still be under the kitchen sink," he told me. "If we're very lucky."

I found the string. I cut it into right-size lengths. I bundled the first batch of the millions of papers and carried them out to the curb. I came back in and bundled more. Two more trips; then I sat and rested, swiped the sweat off my face. After a while Granddad slept, and I was a little out of breath from bundling. I got myself a glass of ice water from the chaos kitchen and went back into the room where Granddad was; told myself I was keeping watch, though in actual fact I was resting.

You still friends with that boy next door? I thought of the question, and I knew the answer: Of course I was. Of course. Even if he was the most mysterious guy in the whole tenth-going-into-eleventh grade. A guy Rocco had been calling Clam ever since fourth grade. A guy Leisha used to say was hers, except he never said it back. I was still friends with Nick Burkeman, because I'd known him the longest.

He'd moved in next door halfway through my first-grade year, back when I still had a dad. He was an only child too, and his mom had a thing for TV, and our backyards shared a couple of big trees between them. He had these miniature planes he used to fly—paper planes and wooden ones he'd build from kits—and one or the other of them was always escaping, sailing off to the Robertsons' or plunking down into my mother's little squares of outdoor zinnias.

We started being friends when I started rescuing his planes, digging them out from wherever they crashed and walking them back through the trees so that Nick could fix them up again. One day he said that I could help him make them fly. The next day I said I wanted to. And we were friends like that—flying planes, but hardly talking—and sometimes climbing trees together and sometimes climbing out onto Nick's flat roof to look at the stars, the birds, the clouds, the real planes, the smoke the real planes left behind. He hardly talked, but he didn't have to. He started talking less when he went to work, after school and on the weekends, for JB's Automotive.

You still friends with that boy next door? Granddad had asked, and maybe *friends* was the hardest and funniest of words. Maybe *friends* wasn't something I talked about. Maybe I was friends with Nick, but maybe it should have been more.

FIVE

THAT NIGHT rain was threatening. I yanked the screen door tight at Granddad's house so it wouldn't flap off its hinges. The sky was a spool of dark cotton candy, and the windows in the apartments above the stores had been pulled shut. There weren't many cars on the street, not many people; all the temporary sidewalk signs and bargain tables were plainly out of sight. I felt little spits of rain, then nothing. I felt a breeze, and then the clouds got thin where the moon was. And then the moon got lost again behind the cotton candy, and the wind blew harder, and there was a brisk, white snap of lightning. Right from the place where the sky had broken poured buckets and buckets of rain.

I was closest to Pastrami's, and so I pressed against its door, hunched beneath the overhang and against the purple neon squiggle that spelled BAGELS, which is another Pastrami's special, bagels sweet as doughnuts and jeweled up with seeds, poppies being my favorite kind. I had flip-flops on, a denim skirt, and a halter top, and the hair that I'd pulled back into one of my mother's tortoise-shell claws had gotten loose and tangled. I saw a man run by, holding a briefcase above his head like a slickened black shelf. I saw the feet and the legs of a man and a woman beneath the dome of an umbrella. Down the road in the railroad tunnel a handful of com-muters took shelter, and there a boy, impatient, with a bike. I thought I heard that mongrel barking. I thought I heard someone crying in a second-story room above my head. The rain made the sound of people clapping.

I thought about Granddad back on his couch, the newspapers I'd bundled and carried out to the street curb for the recyclers, how all those days would become one day in the soggy mess of the rainstorm. I wondered if the rain would sound louder now that I'd made his place more hollow. "Just the tip of the iceberg," he'd said after I'd knotted the last bundles tight. And then he told me to go straight home so that I could beat the storm.

But it had come on quick, and it was falling fierce, and there was no point in going back to Granddad's house, but there wasn't much point in rushing home either. I was drenched up to my knees, and the hem of my skirt was rain soaked too, and whenever the wind blew, the rain slanted in, toward Pastrami's. A long train pulled into the station across the way, and first the passengers stood in the door to the train as if they were going nowhere, and then they shot down the metal stairs and slopped through the puddles, fighting with broken umbrellas. Maybe my mother was already home, and if she was, would she be watching for me through her windows?

Another crack of lightning unzipped the sky. Another roar of thunder answered. The rain fell heavier and harder, and there was a bigger crowd in the railroad tunnel, and the few cars there were threw sheets of rainwater sideways in the glare of the headlights. I don't know how long I stood in the shelter of Pastrami's or how long it took before the rain lost its power, turning into something spritzy. But it was only then, after the storm had gone soft, that I once again heard music playing. I stepped out from beneath Pastrami's and looked diagonally across the street.

There was hardly any light at the dance

studio, but in the dim illumination I saw a woman with candy red hair in a tight-fitting black Lycra dress. She was working the air as if the air were silk, and behind the streaks of rain she disappeared and returned and blurred and bent, and I could not see a partner. It was just the woman and the mirror and the windows streaked with rain, just the woman, turning and snatching, and lifting one arm, and making two of herself in the mirror.

I heard the boy with the bike pedaling up from the tunnel. I saw the tunnel people slowly dispersing. There were more cars on the road, sloshing the deep puddles sideways, and still the dancer kept dancing, wrapping herself up with her one arm, then spinning and unspooling. She did the same thing over and again, as if she had made some sort of deal with herself: so many repetitions, so many spins, so many tosses of the right hand. She spun out of sight, came back, then vanished.

The place went dark. *Wait*, I thought. *Come back.* But she was gone, and when I was sure that she was absolutely gone, I started running home through the tunnel, lifting my arms beneath the clouds that were slowly getting lighter.

"Is that you, Rosie?" my mother called when she heard me shut our door.

"Just me," I said.

She came halfway down the steps, took one long stare at my streaming dark hair, tucked her own behind a porcelain ear. "You're soaking wet," she said.

"There was a storm," I told her.

"What you need, Rosie Keith, is a warm shower."

"I know," I said, and when her back was turned, I did a quick turn in the shadows.

SIX

GRANDDAD TRIPLE STACKED HIS BOOKS, and in peculiar places between his books he'd stuffed papers and ribbons and things. He said it was his personal filing system, and when I asked him how I was supposed to know what to keep and what to toss, he said, "When you get to be in my condition, you don't keep things for yourself. You let somebody else decide what should be held in trust." He had asked me to focus on the in-between things. The books we'd get to later.

"We should ask Mom," I said.

"You're here," he said. "She's not."

"But how am I supposed to know what any of it means?" I asked, shaking an old envelope out of a book of Shakespeare sonnets. A crust of something flowerish plopped out from some fat textbook: crunchy, old, and gray. A package of seeds slipped from a dictionary. An old ketchup bottle label dropped out from *The Old Man and the Sea*. "I read this book," I said, holding up the Hemingway so that Granddad could see.

"A classic," he said. "Built to last." He was sitting upright on his couch with Riot asleep on his lap. He had put on his glasses, which made his eyes look even bigger than they were, more watery, like pools.

"You didn't answer my question."

"I forget your question."

I punched my free fist into my hip and turned back to his shelves. From between the pages of poetry slid a feather, red and puffy. "How," I said, saying each word slowly, "am I

38

supposed to know what any of that stuff *means*?"

"Oh," he said. "That's simple. Ask."

I stared at him. I waited. I was learning about Granddad that he could be 100 percent exasperating, and maybe he liked being that way, or maybe that came from the cancer. The front part of his pure white hair had fallen down across his face. With his hand he pushed it back. I could see all his finger bones, as if there weren't even any skin, and I thought about what Mom had said about the cancer's starting in a place that nobody could see, and how it was his back that had ached at first, how it had hurt to work his garden, to ride his old bike with the basket, but he'd ignored it. Ignored it and then, when he'd found out what was wrong, done what he could to fight it, something called thalidomide, another thing called corticosteroids. But that had been three years ago, and the cancer had come back, and now it was too far gone to catch it. "I'm all through fighting," he had told my mother, but that didn't stop her from arguing with him or from trying to hide her sadness.

"That feather?" he said at last. "That feather has meaning."

"Yeah?" I turned back toward him and shifted on my feet. "What kind?"

"It was a feather on a dress."

"A dress?"

"Not my dress."

"Couldn't have been Riot's." The Maine coon opened her eyes when she heard her name. She stood and padded Granddad's khaki pants, then wrapped herself back up into a fur ball.

"Red," he said softly, "was your grand-mother's color."

I tried to imagine the sort of dress to which such a feather might belong. Tried to imagine a woman with feathers for a neck, or for a hem, who said red belonged to her, tried to picture Granddad with that woman, young.

"Aideen had such style," Granddad said, drawing circles over the head of Riot with his hand. "She was always the star of the show." He said nothing else, just sat as if he'd forgotten I was there: I, his one and very only granddaughter. The windows in his living room were open. A mellow breeze was blowing through, and also the zoom of cars and the sound of someone across the street, whistling some tune. The feather felt like nothing in my hand. I had to keep my eye on it to be sure that it didn't disappear. I waited for Granddad to tell, but his mind had traveled and I was still stuck in a room full of things that were old and mysterious.

"I'm putting the feather In Trust," I said, after a while, placing it on the coffee table beneath a book of poems. I left a puffy corner sticking out, so that I would not forget it later.

"Good decision." He didn't open his eyes.

"Are you getting hungry?"

"Tired more than hungry."

"You can sleep, you know."

"I'm becoming a champion sleeper," he said.

"Do you want the windows shut?"

"I'm starting to like the sound of that guy's whistle." He let his head fall back against the cushion. His hand stopped drawing halos over Riot's puffy head. The point of his chin dropped low toward his neck. His head began to bob, then stilled. The only thing alive about him was the coming in and blowing out of his breath.

I spent the rest of the afternoon shaking the pages of all those volumes loose, sorting the fragments and bits. A lot of the time a book had been made thick with a tear of newspaper that cracked when I tried to unfold it. I wondered whether Granddad even remembered any of this stuff. I thought maybe he was like a squirrel, burying the green walnuts in autumn so that they could rot come spring.

But he had left the sorting up to me; that was my job, and after a while I had a system involving three of the baskets that had been stacked up by the TV. One was for In Trust. One was for Toss. One was for Deciding Later. A whole wad of stuff showed up in the D.L. at first, to buy me thinking time. I tossed old newspaper stories because news belongs to anyone. I tossed old labels, the buds of flowers that had turned brown, bookmarks that seemed to have been set aside for their usefulness and not for any kind of beauty. Into In Trust I put the feather and a stash of antique coins and braided ribbons and buttons and even embroidered collars taken from old clothes. I put decks of photographs that had somehow melted, one picture into the other, photos I'd one day steam apart. I put postcards and letters that someday I'd read. I put pressed leaves when the leaves still looked like nature. I put recipe cards on which were written the secrets to favorite pasta sauces, lists of exotic spices, best-sounding desserts from foreign places, a list of favorite herbs. I put whatever looked like something I could hold on to later, whatever I thought might tell a story about a man who had loved and lost and dreamed adventure but never traveled far.

Outside, the day got warmer, and inside, the sun changed places in the room. The triangle of heat that had been spilled against the floor was now spilled across the couch where Granddad sat, turning the tallest fuzz of Riot's fur gold and pouring a splash of almost orange across Granddad's chest and chin. He had hardly moved since he'd fallen asleep. The whistler was gone, and now there were so many different sounds outside that I couldn't tell one from another. It wasn't silence, but it felt like silence. It felt like being alone.

I needed a chair to reach the shelves that held the highest stuff. I grabbed the nearest one, stood up there, and collected my balance, and now I shook the past out of the books up high, until I got to the stash of old black vinyls—records inside cardboard sleeves that spelled the names of artists. I'd heard of some. Frank Sinatra. Charlie Parker. Sammy Davis Jr. Benny Goodman. Duke Ellington. The Count Basie Orchestra. Ella Fitzgerald. Johnny Mercer. Irving Berlin.

The cardboard sleeves were beat up, and the pictures were faded, and if I was ever to free the songs on them, I'd have to fix the old record player. Still, I knew that these were In Trust treasures. That music was part of my granddad's mystery. That this music could bring back parts of his past. I pulled the records from the shelves, three and four at a time. I piled them beside the coffee table. I felt sweat roll down my neck, saw Riot give me one of her most suspicious looks.

Granddad never woke back up that day; he was still sleeping when I left. I poured a tall glass of water over lots of chunks of ice and put it right where he would find it. I set a bowl of pretzels beside the water, in case he changed his mind about food. I wrote him a note that said, "Coming back tomorrow." Then I kissed the tallest two fingers of my right hand and pressed them to his forehead.

"Mom?" I called when I got home.

But there wasn't any answer.

SEVEN

ONCE I FOUND MYSELF SPYING on Mr. Paul and my mother. It wasn't done on purpose. I'd gone to Leisha's house, seven blocks and a better neighborhood away from mine, to work on some social studies project called Seeing. This was in our ninth-grade year, and Leisha and I were project partners. The purpose of the exercise was to gather evidence about the so-called human condition, to come up with a list of things that make us one connected species. Leisha and I sat around for a while, eating extra-hot

Doritos, and then we set off for a walk up and down the streets of Leisha's neighborhood. Being tall and model thin, Leisha's not afraid of strutting. She has a spray of freckles over milky chocolate skin, wears hats to keep her color fast. When you go walking with Leisha, you walk with style. You know she'll tell you what she sees from where she sees it, which is up high.

So we'd gone out that day, for the sake of Mr. Marinari's class. We'd gone through streets of old houses scrubbed up to look like new and down a short, squat strip of beige-ugly condos, and we had a lot of things on our list that we'd seen: gardens, little Do Not signs, fences, rocking chairs on porches, and big TVs, all of which said something or other about people's needs.

It was a good-enough list, but not a great one. By then we'd gone maybe five blocks north of Leisha's house to a street of mis-matched architecture: turrets on some houses; cinder blocks for some garages; a brand-new mini McMansion faced with stucco between two old-time ugly ranches. Leisha was doing her reporting from up high, tattling out random sights, as if she were peering in through so many frosty snow globes: *Woven doilies over couches. Posters in thin frames. Cat on sill. All-alone boy playing with toy. Old man and even older woman in total-vomit red-plaid room. Empty flower vase.* All of which I was taking down in the notebook we'd brought along for that purpose, until Leisha said, "Oh, my God," then nothing.

"What?" I said, but Leisha was stuck on the sidewalk, saying nothing else, just staring.

So I stared where she was staring, toward a perfectly ordinary house: brown brick, black shutters, concrete square of a stoop, no real doodads I could see, nothing for our Seeing list. Then I looked through the afternoon glare past the window into the ordinary

49

living room, and that's when I saw what Leisha had seen: my own mother and Mr. Paul, taking a break from window washing. My mom in her overalls and Mr. Paul in his, mashing his fat lips to hers. My mom still had one of her tangerine-colored gloves on. She had herself so up against him that there was no air between them.

"I thought," Leisha said, "that Mr. Paul was—"

"Yeah," I said, "he is."

"I thought your mom was—"

"Don't ask me about my mother," I said. "I don't have the first idea."

"I thought—"

"Forget it, Leisha. Forget it, okay?" I started walking fast, but Leisha just stayed put, staring and staring. I went back and yanked at her skinny arm until she started moving. "We're a whole honking lot of out of here," I said. "Got it?"

"But—" she said.

"And you didn't see that, right?"

"Whatever. Sure."

"No buts," I said, "and no whatevers." And don't even ask me what I never wrote down on that list that cataloged our shared human condition.

EIGHT

SOMETHING YOU CAN RELY ON is Pastrami's water ice. Cherry and lemon and Welch's colored grape, for a dollar fifty, sold middle of May straight through September. They scoop it like ice cream into a paper cone, and they give you a spoon and three totally recycled napkins, and if you need to change the flavor of your day, you order yourself up one. It was getting past five in the afternoon. I'd been at Granddad's forever. Mom had put ten dollars on the kitchen counter before she'd left for work in the so much earlier morning, saying, "Don't count on me for dinner." That's it. Period. Not even an "I'm sorry."

"Don't worry," I didn't say back.

Granddad had been getting tired. He had told me several different versions of how I should be on my way, but I had nothing and nobody to go home to and nothing to lose by savoring every single spoonful of Pastrami's grape ice. Mr. D'Imperio himself had scooped out my cone, giving me extra for free, telling me how you had to feed the corporation, which was his fancy way of designating the stomach. "How's your grandfather?" he'd asked me, and I'd simply said, "Fine," and he'd said, "You tell him Mr. D. says hi," and I'd said that I would, tomorrow.

"You won't forget now, will you, Rosie?"

"I forget nothing," I said, which was hardly a lie.

"A chip off the old block," said Mr. D.

"Which block?" I wanted to know.

53

"Grandfather's block on your mother's side," Mr. D. answered. He was holding his stomach as he sometimes did, as if it needed the bracing of his hands to keep it high. "We go back," he said, "a very long time."

I nodded.

"I never knew your grandfather to forget a thing," he said.

"Doesn't throw much away either," I said. I felt my face go hot, despite the ice, but Mr. D. was not offended; he just laughed his big it-all-begins-at-the-stomach laugh.

"You're all spice, Rosie," he told me.

I nodded again, as if I were sure that spice was the best possible thing you could be. "Good batch of grape ice," I said, backing up toward the door.

"We have it all summer long at Pastrami's."

By now I was out in the late sun, standing with my back against the redbrick wall that divided Pastrami's from Whiz Bang. The road was rush-houred over with cars and trucks.

Peak-hour trains came and went. Sidewalks on either side were overwhelmed with walkers. I was nothing to anyone passing by, as see-through as an early shadow, and I was thinking of Leisha at the shore, and I was thinking about Nick working the innards of cars, and I was thinking about Rocco on his ten-step program to get smart. I was thinking as well about how I myself was not having what you'd call a typical teenage summer, but then again, I thought, how many summers actually are? How many summers aren't in some secret way lonely?

The grape ice had sent a fist of cold to the right side of my head. I twirled what was left with my spoon and drank it down. Time, I thought, to be on my way. Time. I tossed the paper cone and the plastic spoon into a trash receptacle and found my place inside the rush-hour crowd, which was mostly streaming the opposite way, back toward Granddad's, making a hot burst of wind.

I began to focus on the little in-between places inside the commotion: the single halves of strangers' cell phone talk; the wedges of nothing in and around people's shoulders; the mini puzzle pieces of undisturbed air; the things that didn't move set against all the things that did. I remembered my envy of Leisha's height, her special way of seeing. And then I tilted my own eyes high, to find a slice of sky. That was how I discovered the cluster of balloons—the bobbing silver, white, and pink with the sunbeams trapped inside.

They could have been clouds, scraping close to earth. They could have been poppies after they'd bloomed or tears on the face of the moon. They had that gleam inside them, and there were maybe eight or ten, knocking softly against one another above a pair of legs that I noticed only after the legs had left the crowd and crossed, a diagonal northwest, to the other side of the street. The legs, the balloons went west. They stopped at the door to a studio above and cut in away from the street.

I followed the white, the silver, the pink. I came to the studio door. I pushed through. There was a flight of stairs up: very long, very narrow. There were brownish-reddish–colored walls. There were photographs of dancers—aquamarine and yellow and red gowns, men in black tuxedos—on every available wall. "House of Dance," a bright painted poster said. *House of Dance.* I stood there undetected, listening to the music and the throb, the very slight and very sweet bobbing together of balloons.

NINE

AFTERWARD, WHEN IT was getting past dusk and my mother hadn't yet come home, I picked up the pink Princess phone my father had once sent me with a note, "Call anytime." Yeah. Right. I carried the phone to the center of my bed, sat down, and dialed Leisha's cell, even though she was what she called an emergency cell phone user, which no girl in Somers High or perhaps the whole world could understand except for me. Leisha's an in-person kind of friend. She's a big hit or miss on the phone. But I was lonely, and I took a chance, and after five long rings she answered, a little out of breath.

"Leisha," I said, "it's me."

"Hi, you." I could picture her with her hair falling down around her shoulders, a T-shirt on, a pair of silky shorts cut high on her long, lovely legs. She might have been smoothing after-sun butter lotion on, or polishing her toenails with her signature color, which is dark purple tending toward black. She might have been finishing a bowl of orange sherbet, which was something she had almost every night and never gained an ounce.

"How are the little terrors?" I asked.

"Rotten," she said. "Want to know *how* rotten? Jake managed to get his head stuck in a sand bucket today. Yanked the thing on like a marching-band hat and then couldn't get it off. Had to take him back to the house to cut him free, and he screamed every step of the way."

"Pretty," I said.

"Totally Jake," she said. "Thank God no one I know is down here." She was whispering, so I had the phone pressed hard against my ear. I imagined her turned away from where everyone else was, curled around the secret of our conversation in a house at the beach where the air outside smelled like breeze and the air inside was all damp towels and little-boy screams and clumps of sand. "Lucky for you," she said, "that you're cousin free."

"I guess," I said.

"Then again," she said, "there's this lifeguard. Totally and completely hot. Take Nick and times him by a hundred."

"Do you talk to him?"

"No, I don't talk to him. I just look at him, and that's enough." I pictured Leisha down at the beach with her perfect model body. If she'd seen the guy, then he'd seen her. There was no doubting that.

"So what's with you?" she said. "What's up?"

"I wanted . . ." I began, and then I didn't know where to start, how to explain how my summer was going, what it was that I felt, why I'd called in the first place when I had to know that she would be busy, that she wouldn't have the time to talk. "My grand-dad's been sick," I said fast. "And my mother's my mother. And Nick is never home. Stuff." I wanted to tell Leisha about the House of Dance and the balloon bouquet. About the dancers I'd seen through the window. About my grandfather reading magazines on places he would never ever get to. "Music and throb," I wanted to say, but that would have been stupid, so I still kept hunting for words, and then, before I knew what words to use, all hell was letting loose.

"Oh, my God," Leisha said, whispering no more.

"What?" I could hear crashing and scampering, someone bawling his eyes out.

"I think Jake's just flushed his brother's

swimsuit down the toilet."

"You're kidding me."

"No. I'm not. Oh. My. God. It never ends. I have to go, Rosie. I'm sorry."

"Eight more weeks and we're juniors together," I said.

"Heaven," she said. "Compared to this." It was getting louder and louder where she was. As if she were taking a walk in a zoo right around feeding time.

I hung up the phone, and the skies were dark. I lay down and hoped that I would fall asleep sooner than I could start to cry.

TEN

THE VERY LAST TIME I saw my father, he was standing in the shadows. There was the bigness of a moon shining in through my bedroom windows, but all I saw was half of his face and the thumb that he was pressing to his earlobe. He thought I was asleep, and even though I was pretty sure he was leaving for good—I had heard what he had said; I had heard my mother crying—that's what I let him think, that I was asleep, because he didn't deserve to know how much I was going to miss him.

My father was a big, tall guy and half Italian, and he was more celebrity than anything else, made you feel as big and special as he was when he was in the room. Then he'd leave and wouldn't come home for days, and he'd make you feel forgotten. When I was little, I told Nick, Leisha, and Rocco that he was an astronaut. I told them that he rode elephants in India. I told them that he was digging up a new Egyptian mummy. I told them that he was far too famous to spend much time at home. But when he left for good, I told them nothing except that life was better without him. "More room for me in my house" is what I said, and my very best friends made like they believed me.

The first year was the hardest: the first birthday of mine, the first birthday of Mom's, the first Thanksgiving, the first Christmas. Granddad would come, but my mother still was crying or about to start crying, tears streaking down her face and globbing her mascara. I think it was after Christmas when Granddad started to say that it was time that Mom moved on, that life was to be lived, that there was a big wide world to see, and maybe, he said, my father's running off had been some kind of hidden blessing. My mom didn't appreciate that, not at all. "You never liked him," she would answer, "so don't pretend you understand."

"I know something about loss," he'd say, "and I know something about not living."

"Mom never stopped loving you," Mom would say. "My loss is bigger. My loss is learning that everyone else is loved more than you are. Don't think you know what I'm going through or that you can make it better."

"You're young, Jeanine," he'd say. "Trust me."

"I'm all through trusting," she'd say. "He left. He didn't want me."

"Where are you going to get, feeling sorry for yourself?"

"Where did you ever get, Dad? Think about it. Where did you ever go?"

She'd stomp upstairs, her little body making hippo sounds, her crying avalanching down from the top of the stairs, from her room. She'd leave Granddad with me, and it was like a scene in a show that you could count on happening until Granddad just plain stopped coming by. He made like he lived a million miles away, even though he's been walking distance since forever.

The next day, when I came home from Granddad's, I was betting on the house's being empty, betting that Mom would be somewhere with Mr. Paul, holding on to her new idea of happiness. I put my key into the lock, but the lock was already popped. I pushed wide the door, and the lights were on. I heard low talk, and guessing now what I was about to find, I followed its sound. I found them together in the kitchen—he stirring something with a spoon in a pot on the

66

burner, she standing beside him with her chin on the ledge of his shoulder. Mr. Paul was not a big man, and he wasn't handsome either. He had overalls on over a navy-blue T-shirt, sandals on his feet. On the parts of his head where hair still grew he had buzzed it short.

"Have a good day?" I asked, louder than necessary, so I could freak out my mom, who had not heard me come in.

"Rosie," she said when she turned. "Well. Hello, Rosie. Mr. Paul is making pasta." She scuttled away from him as if she were stacked on crab legs and touched a finger to an itch beneath her chin.

"Uh-huh." I folded my arms across my chest and stood there solid, looking straight into her eyes, which were, I suddenly noticed, a lot like Granddad's. She combed one hand through her long black hair and stared back at me, practically pleading.

"You hungry, Rosie?"

"Nope."

"You want to sit with us?"

She didn't mean it, and I didn't budge: "I'm busy."

"Did you say hello to Mr. Paul?" Mom asked, because now he had turned too, was stirring the pot behind his back, as if pasta couldn't be left for just one minute.

"How's the window-washing business?" I asked very fake politely.

"It's our busy season," he said.

"I bet."

"Couldn't keep up with all the demand without your mother."

"Yeah. She's something."

"Really, Rosie. There's plenty of pasta. If you want to join us."

"Ate already."

"Well, that's good, I guess."

"It was more than good. It was delicious."

My mother gave me a look that said "Please please please don't mortify me, Rosie," begged me with her eyes. But the mean part of me was already loose, and I was fighting a little urge to ask Mr. Paul about his wife. "Is she waiting on you for supper?" I wanted to say. "Is she thinking she's forgotten? Does she even have any idea that you've stopped loving her?" I had a million ways that I could ask it, but I held my tongue. I took my time walking over to the pantry and pulling myself out a box of saltines and a jar of peanut butter. "For later," I said, and I turned on my heels and took the stairs, two by two, up to my room. I slammed the door behind me, as loud as a door can be slammed. I sat down on one corner of my bed. I inhaled and exhaled, inhaled and exhaled so my heart would stop beating so fast. I didn't know at whom I was maddest—my dad for leaving, my mom for needing, or Mr. Paul for taking advantage. I didn't know for whom I felt sorriest: Mrs. Paul or me or my mother, all being messed with by a loser.

I unscrewed the lid on the peanut butter

jar and dug the shovel of a saltine in, dug in another and then another, letting the crumbs snow all over my bed. I tried not to listen to the putting down of plates and the pulling out of chairs for the dinner down below. *Whatever*, I thought. *Whatever*. Because it was not like anyone was asking me if I wanted the bald one around.

After a while my mouth was peanut glue and the saltines were like cardboard. I stood to check on the moon, which wasn't that full and wasn't that close. I opened the window and closed my eyes and tried to hear the music from the House of Dance, but in between me and the dancers there were cars and trains, and houses and people and their sorrows, and coughing and silence, and TV and romance, and things lost and stolen. I couldn't hear the throb at the House of Dance. But I could hear Mr. Paul and my mother laughing, puffs of sweetened ha-ha stuff inside mumbled conversation. My mom was laughing, but she didn't mean it. I knew precisely how her laughter sounded when she felt glad or lucky.

Back when he was ours, my dad had a knack for making Mom and me feel lucky. Because we'd been chosen by him. Because he was so handsome. Because nobody told his kind of stories. We didn't have to have anything else if we had him, that's how lucky he made us, and if he carried me on his shoulders, I could touch the sun, and if he said "RosieRosieRosie," I knew the melody of my own name, and if I did something that made him smile, then I was blessed and lucky, both. But lucky, Mom said, after he'd gone for good, was no kind of blessing. Lucky was the taste of something sweet that had already been swallowed.

Mom wanted nothing lucky from right then on, which is the best way I have of explaining Mr. Paul. She'd answered an ad: "Window Washer Wanted." Good with rags and a bucket, I guess. Good with breakable things. Good at coming and going, not being noticed, good at standing on top of a ladder, nothing, I'm telling you, nothing the least bit lucky about it. "You take what you're given, and when nobody's giving, you take what you can get," she'd said. I remember that because I was eleven. Because lucky for me had become Leisha and Nick, and also Rocco, when he wasn't being stupid. Lucky was having my mom all to myself before she fell for Mr. Paul. I'd just thought that she'd gone off to make some money. I didn't know that she was about to achieve her own brand of leaving too, that it would be up to me to fix my family's sorrows.

You want to know how I know how long I've been abandoned by my celebrity dad? I keep a running count of all his twenties. That night I had 385, no more, no less, which, in money speak, equals $7,700. The week after that I'd have 386. One week more, and—the math could not be more no-brainer; even Rocco, his mighty self, could do it. The shoe box behind the crate of toys was getting explosively full.

What difference could it possibly make if I dug in to relieve the pressure?

Who was going to notice?

ELEVEN

THREE DAYS LATER, approaching Granddad's, I heard voices that I deciphered
at first as coming from TV. But then again, I
thought, Granddad's clunker didn't work;
besides, the closer I got, the plainer it was
that one of the voices was Granddad's. I
could hear him clear as anything as I walked
through his kitchen door. I could hear him
talking about cranberry juice, the newest best
drink, he was saying, for morning.

"Granddad?" I called.

"Right here, Rosie," he answered, as if I

wouldn't know by then where to find him. I walked through the kitchen and into the dining-living-bookshelves room, and there he was, and there was Riot, and there she was, a stranger. She had big brown eyes, and a braid of color on one wrist that could have been a tattoo; her white shirt made her skin seem darker. Her hair was long and like my mother's hair—the color of black ink and silky—and she was standing much too near my grandfather, holding a tall glass with a little stain of cranberry color at the bottom. She'd stuffed a pillow into the place beneath one of his arms—a bigger, fatter pillow than the one he'd had before. "This is Teresa," Granddad finally introduced her.

"Teresa," I said.

"And this," he said, indicating me with his chin, "is Rosie."

"Your granddad's been telling me about you," Teresa said, her words coming out decorated with some kind of lacy, sweet accent.

Indian? Turkish? Moroccan?

"Teresa is here to help," Granddad said, and as if to prove it, she fitted the new pillow to the place behind his head, patted it down until he settled against it. Riot, in her wicker basket, stood up, stretched, and mewed.

"I thought *I* was here to help," I said, looking at Granddad and then at Teresa; knotting my arms tight across my chest. All of a sudden I was feeling fierce inside, because wasn't I just starting to figure things out, and did I really need this, some other kink in my messed-up family system? Defense or offense? What was called for? Who was whose, and what was I?

"There are different kinds of help, Rosie," Granddad said. He was looking fresh, with a pair of clean pants on, a clean white shirt, fresh-shaven face. Better—okay, I admit it—than he'd looked with just me around.

"I'm your granddad's nurse," Teresa said. "To help"—she nodded toward him—"your granddad." She said it in her up-and-lilting accent, looking at me steady as a nurse is steady, not the tiniest, speckiest dust of self-confidence lacking, even though she'd told me nothing new.

"You need a nurse?" I said to Granddad, through tight lips that stopped me from saying anything more. I knew it shouldn't have come as a surprise to me, I knew that he was dying, but I also knew that he couldn't die soon, that we had plenty of cleaning and sorting to do, that I needed time, that we were granddaughter-grandfather, and that came— had to come—first. I didn't like what I was seeing.

"Rosie." Granddad said my name, real quiet, in a warning way.

"I was just finished," Teresa said, smiling her extremely white smile. She snapped shut the black vinyl case that had been sitting on the dining room table. She told Granddad she'd see him soon enough. He said he wasn't absconding. "Absconding?" She didn't know the word.

He said, "Absconding. Running off." She laughed. Then she told me to have a good day, and I did not return the favor, and I waited until I heard the kitchen door close. I beamed my most peeved look at Granddad.

"Teresa is doing her job," he said. "There was no reason to be rude."

"You could have told me."

"You're earlier than usual. I thought that she'd be gone before you got here."

"Is she supposed to be a secret?"

"No. But she's not supposed to concern you." He settled even more deeply against his pillow and closed his eyes for a spell.

"What country is she from?" I demanded.

Behind closed eyes he answered: "Teresa was born in the south of Spain."

"Is that a real tattoo on her wrist or a fake one?"

"Well, that's something to ask her."

"How many words doesn't she know?"

"You're full of interesting questions."

"Did you tell her about In Trust?" I asked.

"That's for you to do, if you want to." He opened his eyes and gave me the look that said he was done with talk for a while. I looked past him, toward the pile of things that I was supposed to be sorting. Truth was I had hardly made a dent. I'd been sitting around, mostly, talking mostly, and there were still piles of things on windowsills, tabletops, shelves, still big old parts and pieces of whatever sitting on his floor, still a lot of stuff in the old D.L. Maybe my lack of doing had made a nurse like Teresa obligatory. Maybe if I'd done a better job, I'd still have Granddad all to myself.

"How'd you get yourself a southern Spanish nurse?" I asked.

"The gods of fortune, I guess." He smiled behind his eyes, still closed.

"How often will she be coming?"

"When I need her, which will be often, Rosie. And those are just the facts."

"You still need me, though, right?" I asked.

"Yes."

"Do you know if your stereo works?"

"My stereo?"

"That thing. I mean, all the pieces of that thing. On the floor beside you. Here." I pointed to the mess.

He didn't lean over the couch to look. He didn't even open his eyes. He just nodded, slowly. "That's an antique, Rosie. They don't even make those anymore."

"Yeah. But does it work?"

"Well, I can't say that it's broken."

"When's the last time you used it?"

"When I put a song on for Aideen."

"So I can mess with it? You don't mind?"

"Whatever's mine," he said, "is yours."

He slept then, and I sat on the floor near him, pulled the turntable and the amps and the speakers and the cables out to where I could get a better look. The clear plastic lid on the turntable had a thick, snowy layer of dust that I half blew off, half rubbed away with the bottom of my old Dippy Don's T-shirt. Beneath the lid was the round, flat part that you put the records on, also some knobs, a long silver arm with a needle that I could only hope still had sufficient scratch, and a name: Sansui Automatic Return/Shut-off. The speakers were the size and shape of a Cheez-It cracker box. The cables had yellow ends, red ends, white ends, prongs. The amp was pretty much just a black box with holes in the back that had been shaped to fit the cables.

The first thing that I had to figure out was what connected to what, which wasn't going to be easy. I tried every combination I could think of until I found the working one, until the speakers seemed to hum when I held them to my ear and all the dust there had been had been blown off the silver needle. I didn't know what time it was or whether Granddad was still sleeping. I didn't know whether the records in those sleeves could still give up their songs.

"Here goes nothing," I said to myself. I made my way to the album pile, chose the one with the cover that had lots of brightly colored squares and a name that seemed right for the day: *What Kind of Fool Am I*. I tipped that record out of its sleeve, fitted it onto the turntable, and dialed the turntable to on. Like a dinosaur bird waking up from sleep, the arm with the needle lifted and, slowly, slowly, shook toward the spinning record, hung above it creakily, and then dropped. There were a couple of seconds of absolute fuzz, the sound ginger ale makes after it's poured over ice, as the needle slid from the slippery black edge in toward the grooves. And then there was music and a man singing, little pops and crackles, but mostly a song and the record still spinning and the needle still riding the grooves. I fell back against the side of Granddad's couch, 100 percent amazed by what I'd done.

"Sammy Davis Jr.," I heard Granddad say after a while. "Voice of an angel."

"Brought to you," I said, still on the floor below him, "by Rosie, the one and only."

"I guess that's right."

"No shit, Sherlock," I said. "That *is* right. It wasn't going to play all by itself."

"You watch your language, Rosie," he said, but hardly meant it.

Granddad didn't say anything more until the first song was through. "Pick up the needle, will you, Rosie?" he told me then. "The next song has a scratch straight through it. Used to drive your grandmother crazy. 'Once in a Lifetime,' one of Sammy's best, and we always had to skip it."

"Fine," I said. "But how do I find the next song?"

"Smooth bands between grooved ones. Shows the spaces in between."

I lifted the needle arm and pushed it sideways, to where the bands were smooth again. As carefully as I could, I lowered the needle back in. "'A Lot of Livin' to Do,'" Granddad said, giving the next song its title. "Another classic."

The song was crackly and soupy but had a nice blue ribbon of a tune running through. "How old is this stuff?" I wanted to know.

"Dark Ages," he said. "Born and bred in the year nineteen hundred and sixty-two. Same year as your mother was born. Music like this kept her from crying. Instant cure."

I squeezed my eyes shut and tried to bring to mind my mother, small. Tiniest thing in a white wicker basket. Blanket wrapped around her tight. Little squints for eyes. Whole life ahead of her for real. No lousy celebrity husband in sight. No me. "Who was this guy?" I asked Granddad.

"A Rat Packer. One of Sinatra's good friends. What are they teaching in school these days?"

"Not learning this," I said. "For sure."

"The world's on a downhill slide."

By now Sammy Davis Jr. was singing about something called the beguine. Whatever that was, it made Granddad happy. He stayed quiet, but it was a different kind of quiet. I stood up, so that I could see his face. "Why don't you sit right here beside me, Rosie?" he asked, smoothing his hand over the empty part of the corduroy couch. But I was worried about sitting down so close. Worried I could hurt him.

"You want something to drink?" I asked.

"Not now," he said. "Not thirsty."

"Not even cranberry juice?"

"Not even."

"You mind if I get something?

"What's mine is still and always yours."

He smiled a funny, crooked smile and

pulled on one of his very large ears as I went off to the kitchen. By the time I came back, his eyes were closed again, and a song he said was called "Someone Nice Like You" was playing. I stood where I was and closed my eyes too, trying to picture Mom in Granddad's arms, listening to this music, trying to picture the house before it got so crampy with things whose meanings were hidden. Tried to imagine where the music took my granddad in his mind.

"Listen to the words," Granddad said, and I did, listened to Sammy Davis Jr. of 1962 singing about *if*:

"Aideen knew every word," he said when the song was over. "She was always singing."

"Must have been nice," I said.

"She was something," he said.

"Pretty, I bet."

"Oh, yes. She was. And always, always, in motion. Would walk around and around when she was cooking. Would sway side to side when hanging clothes. Was always a couple of steps ahead when we'd walk down to Pastrami's."

"Mr. D. says hi, by the way," I interjected.

"In the beginning was Pastrami's." Granddad smiled his funny smile. Then he went on with his story. "You know what Aideen would do?" he asked.

"No," I said, "I don't."

"She'd roll back the carpet right about where you are and jitterbug the shine off the floor. She'd fox-trot in circles, with the moon as her man. She'd dial up her music loud."

"Sounds like something," I said.

"She could make the porcelains and the paintings tremble. She could dance. Oh, Aideen could dance."

"Red was her color," I said.

He nodded. "You get an A plus, Rosie."

"And you were her very best man."

"I was privileged, Rosie. Despite everything, she liked me. She'd had her other chances, don't you think she didn't. But she stuck around for me."

"You're a likable guy," I said.

"I'm an ordinary guy."

"You're better than fireworks."

"You're a top-drawer liar." His voice was weary.

"I'm putting all the albums In Trust," I told him after he didn't say much more.

"I always took you for a smart one," he answered.

"I'm putting the albums In Trust, even if they all sound like Sammy Davis Jr., even if not one of them, not even one, is nearly as good as Usher."

"Faster or slower. More or less. They've got the Sammy Davis style. Besides," he said, "*usher* is a verb."

"It's also a noun."

"Let's call it versatile."

He had used up most of his voice. There were dots of sweat in the creases on his brow.

"I think you could use a nap," I said.

"I'm getting too tired not to be tired," he said. "I'm sorry."

I came to him, and I settled his pillow. I sat back down to watch him sleep. He closed his eyes and sighed and turned. I listened for the music, then, from far, far down the street. I tried to find my mother in my mind: in a house somewhere, in her overalls, listening to the squeaks of rags on glass. Did she ever think of her growing-up music? Did she ever remember the old-time songs or the feel of the moon on her face?

TWELVE

TWO MONTHS AFTER Leisha and I caught my mother making out with Mr. Paul, Leisha, Nick, Rocco, and I went to the theater in the next town over to see a new James Bond movie. It was Christmastime and bitter cold outside, and we'd gotten a ride from Rocco's mom, who drove a bright-turquoise Pontiac Sunbird from the Jurassic era. Rocco sat up front. Nick sat in back, between Leisha and me, and the window on my side was broken, rolled halfway down and not budging. There were flakes of snow in the wind blowing through. The wind itself was brutal.

I was shivering, and Rocco and Leisha were laughing. Nick, though, didn't laugh, not much, just put his arm around me and pulled me close. "For warmth's sake," he said, and I shiver-nodded yes and leaned against him, leaned in hard, wanting the drive never to end. I knew about throb, is what I'm trying to say, before I found the House of Dance.

But now, coming and going to Granddad's, sitting and waiting at Granddad's, bending and bundling and boxing at Granddad's, I was always on the hunt for something bigger than the work before me, bigger than the facts of Granddad's sickness and my mom's absence. A leaf would pinch itself off a tree and flick and glide in the breeze, and that was something good. Or a butterfly would come from nowhere, skidding in. Or a spider would reach a sidewalk curb and step up, his eight legs a sudden mess, and I would think how funny it was to see a spider dance.

How bigger than life itself.

I started studying the steam rising from the asphalt. I was aware of the clouds blotting out the stars at night and the stars coming right back. I was thinking about living and dying, and secrets, and the shadows being cast by trees, and I was standing beneath awnings on the street where Granddad lived, looking up and watching dancers dance, in the long, wide window bands. Those thin arms rising, those hips in a swivel, those hands reaching, that music coming from, and going to, places far away.

The dance was alive. That was what I knew. The dance was something whole. The dance was hope, and hope was what I needed most of all the summer my granddad died. Hope was what I began to put In Trust, above all other things. Hope, which comes in all the brightest colors.

THIRTEEN

THE NEXT MORNING Mom was still not home. I'd knocked on her bedroom door, and no one had answered. I'd opened the door and found her pillow undisturbed. She was gone and had been gone since the day before, and it was morning, and she hadn't even called. I looked out her bedroom window, and I could hear her in my head: Not a word, Rosie.

Later, down on the kitchen table, I found the note she'd left. "Be good," it said, and I thought: *Be good? Be* good! When you call

Mr. Paul's to fix a date for your cleaning, it is Mrs. Paul with whom you speak. Mrs. Paul, who has two young kids, the father of whom is Mr. Paul. Mrs. Paul, who shares a house with Mr. Paul. "Mom," I said out loud, "come home." As if talking were taking some kind of action.

In the house the windows were streaked gray with old rain. Cobwebs hung from the ceilings like old-lady lace, and there wasn't the slightest bit of gleam. There were loose nails and weaknesses in the floor, places that would crack beneath almost any weight. The house was long and thin, with a front room, followed by a dining room, and over to the right of that a kitchen, and only in the front room were there what you might call interesting things: a spinning wheel, a slouched half couch, two bright cotton beanbag chairs. An old Humpty Dumpty sat against one wall, and inside a cabinet of curious things were a shark's tooth, the polished skull of a pine marten, a leather box from Granada, a found clay face from ancient El Salvador, fossilized fish scales, an egg-shaped kaleidoscope, and two impossibly tiny finch skulls, one still with a fringe of feathers at its beak, all these courtesy of my father's endless travels.

Upstairs there are just two rooms, and in between these rooms there is a bathroom that is a gross-out shade of pink. The people before us liked navy blue. They chose it for the carpets and the trim. Even some of the doors are the American flag version of blue. The only room in the house that isn't scorched by blue is the kitchen, which my mother painted yellow. Did it one year to the day after my father had left for good, which approximates the time she started the windowsill farm of basil and potatoes. Maybe if my mom hadn't gotten so caught up with Mr. Paul, she'd have painted the rest of the house. She'd have made it all as ripe as fruit and put some music on.

She'd have been home, cratering her own pillow.

She'd have been with me, because I'd have been enough, because I alone would not be such a tiring, lonesome thing.

It was the eighth morning of July and finally felt like summer. I pushed all the windows open and the back door too, so the fireflies wouldn't forget me. Granddad had told me, before I'd left the day before, to give myself the next day off. "Teresa is coming, isn't she?" I'd said, and he'd said there were some things she needed extra time to do. I didn't ask him what they were.

So it was early, and then it was ten, then noon, and for a while I watched Mrs. Robertson pinning her husband's black socks to the line, but not her underwear, and then I called Nick Burkeman's house, even though I knew he wouldn't be home. "He's at his father's shop," his mother told me when she picked up on her side; there was a TV on loud in the background. "All day?" I asked. "Until six," she said, hurrying me off. I remembered what Nick had once said about his mom: She'd have preferred a TV family. It was what he'd said one night, when we were out on his roof, testing his hypothesis that chirper birds don't fly at night. We could hear beneath us the fake TV laugh. We could hear Nick's mom talking back to the show. It was dark, but I could see him blushing. "Let's find an owl," I'd said, "and let's forget it."

I could have read, I could have knocked away cobwebs, scrubbed out a sink, written a letter I'd never mail to my lousy cash-peeling excuse of a father, but I had been thinking about living and dying, and time was running out. I yanked at the knob on the navy-blue closet door and pulled the door across the navy-blue napped carpet. I shoved aside the crate of little-girl toys and dug in, at last, to my shoe box of cash.

You cannot buy a man who is dying a single meaningful thing. You can only give him back the life he loved, and wake up his memories.

FOURTEEN

THERE IS A SECOND POSTER in the street lobby at the House of Dance that promises a lesson for free; it hangs there easy enough for the whole world to see. "Take the First One on Us," the words say, over a picture of a slick-haired man and a fish-netted woman all meshed up together.

At two o'clock that very same afternoon I was studying that poster, wearing my best white camisole and my shortest lime green skirt and dangling, from one hand, the high-heeled sandals I had stolen from my mother.

I was standing in that lobby, daring myself to take the steps up and up past the brownish-reddish walls and the photographs and the mirrors that would force me into doing the math on myself: my hair, which isn't as black as my mother's; my skin, which isn't as pale; and my eyes, which I had decided by then had come direct from Granddad, by way of my mom.

You could say this idea I'd had was crazy—not sensible, not smart—but I'd made up my mind and come this far, and now I took a first step up, and then another, paused at the first landing, took the next step up. At the end of the stairs was another glass door that wouldn't be budged without the say-so of a buzzer, and when I got there and hit the black box, it spluttered an answer. I pulled the handle of the door, and I was in.

If Leisha could see me now.

If Nick could.

If only my mother.

It was the colors of a foreign place—yellows, but not bright yellows, oranges mixed with twigs of brown, greens not like new greens but like rubbed-out, used-up ones. There was a couch, and there was a reception desk, and beyond that there were two ways to go: straight down the hall to the dance floor, or to the left, which led to rooms, a hall, a closet, and more dance floor. I could see, from where I stood, the blur-sway of dancing, mirrors on any wall that wasn't windowed, fabric, and breeze.

No one bothered to question me, so I watched: the zigzags of arms and fingers and necks and feet, the bursting-out bloom of a peony on a wrist, the frostinglike swirl of a purple hem, all swooshing by. I could hear talk, but it was just pieces of talk. I could, when I really worked at it, make out phrases: "Back rock, hold. Back rock, hold. Everything straight above your sensor." I had no clue what a sensor was. It wasn't a word used in health class.

Now someone was laughing. Now someone stopped laughing. Now the music was swiped away and replaced with a song that was rising and then falling. The song was made of strings, and fisting up through the strings was piano. "One TWO three. One TWO three," the voice was saying above it. "And not looking at me. And not dropping your shoulders. High on the TWOOOO, and three, and one, and again, this is the waltz. You are the queen. Aristocratic." *The queen*, I thought, *has a sensor*.

Nothing was being stopped for my sake. No one was asking my name. I walked the length of the hall, past a board of names, toward the mirrored walls. I crept closer to the wooden floor, the peony wrist, the elbow hinge, the voice that belonged to the black-haired man, who was all in black—his shoes, his pants, his shirt, each strand of his hair. He was the man I had seen through the window, the man on the poster, and he was stepping back, stepping sideways, stepping forward, turning, turning his partner under his arm, starting again. "TWO, three, and one," he said, and when he said the "TWO," his eyebrows went up and when he said the "three," they fell, but he couldn't have been speaking to his partner with his eyes because her face was pressed away from his. I hadn't seen this one in the window before. She had bleached white-blond hair razored just above her ears. If I'd climbed all those steps thinking dance was romance, I had another lesson coming.

"Give me your hands," the man said, though he already had them. "More pressure. Yes. There it is. Heels first and feet parallel. You know this, Teenie. It's in your muscle memory." He had a square face and a big-screen smile. "Dancing isn't torture," he said.

"It isn't right," she said, finally standing up straight and glaring up at him, then stomping off.

"Closer than it was and getting there," he said.

"I should have it by now."

"It takes time."

"The competition's in two weeks."

"Everything you need to know you know," he said. "You have to trust the music now. You have to trust your partner. Me, Teenie. You have to trust me." He stepped into the miniature room where the music machine was. When he reappeared, more music was playing. He bowed toward her. She came to him. He smiled. She didn't. They began. They whirled. They disappeared from my view, and now it was the woman with the peony on her wrist whom I watched, the doll-sized blonde whose eyelashes were fat, black feathers above her gray eyes. Her partner looked nothing like dance except in the face, which beamed a kind of glory. The hair he had was pulled back into a floppy ponytail, and he wore a faded pink-and-yellow shirt. They were standing in front of one wall of mirrors, and she was doing all the talking.

"Don't pull on me," she was saying. "And don't push. This is only rumba walking. I need room, but I also need tension . . . Knees," she said, "and hips. Small steps. Straight legs. Use the inside of your foot. This is what I want. And not that. This." They stepped back and faced each other, and she began to count, "Slow quickquick slow quickquick slow," until he stepped forward and she stepped back and then to the side, and then something else happened, and they broke apart and she walked, like a pony on a tether.

I felt the air in the room change before I understood how it could have, a blast of heat through the conditioned cool. When I turned to see, I understood that the mirrored wall had split, revealing a panel that turned out to be a door. Through the door came the heat of the day and also a cloud of smoke and also, at last, that red-haired dancer. She was so much smaller than I'd taken her to be, even stacked on dangerous shoes. She could have been twenty or thirty, or Hungarian or Polish, or anything else that I wasn't, and I knew her, and she didn't know me, and I shrugged and said nothing.

Her eyes weren't a color I knew—flecks of blue, flecks of green, flecks of gray, something tropical. She looked at the woman with the peony on her wrist, then came in my direction, bringing the heat of the day, the smell of that smoke.

"Are you here for a lesson?" she wanted to know.

I shrugged, then nodded yes.

"Who's your instructor?" She said her *s* like a *z*. She both *z*-ed and purred her "instructor."

"I saw the sign," I said. "Downstairs. 'First One on Us.'"

"You're looking then to begin? You're a beginner?" I couldn't make myself say one way or the other. I looked into her bright-bird eyes and forced myself to smile.

Now she was dancer-walking on her skyscraper heels back down the hall. Now I was turning to follow, my mother's stolen sandals clanking against each other, my sneakers blowing air out of their side holes. Handing me an old clipboard she'd pulled from the reception desk, she told me to sit and fill in blanks, as if I'd traveled all this way in search of a doctor, in search of a cure.

"You answer these questions," she said, "and I'll book you."

Well, this is crazy, I thought. But I sat down and obeyed her, because what she had said was true. I was looking to begin.

FIFTEEN

T HE CANDY-HAIRED dancer was Marissa. She studied the answers I'd scribbled onto the clipboard page and asked if I had the afternoon open.

I said, "Somewhat."

She said, "Two hours, and there's a lesson block free."

I said that would work with my schedule.

The phone behind the check-in desk rang. She answered. I settled into the leather sofa. Crossed my legs, tugged at my skirt, took a good, long look at my mother's shoes, undid the straps, put the sandals on, kicked my sneakers under the couch, and glanced at the clock. Two hours are like a lifetime when you're waiting for your very first ballroom dance lesson. But then again, there is so much to see.

The other dance students were coming up the steps, buzzing through the door, sitting down on the other end of the couch, and starting to change their shoes, because everyone who came to the House carried a drawstring pouch of special dancing shoes. Even the men had their own leather Cubans, shoes, from what I could tell, that were too tight at the toes and too high in the heels with the thinnest leather soles. I twined my legs to cover my feet, but my borrowed sandals were certifiable proof that I was a first timer.

The students came in twos and ones. Most of the twos were what Marissa called the wedding couples. "How is our wedding couple?" she would greet them. "How many weeks is it now till the matrimony?" When one of the brides-to-be brought not a bag but a box, Marissa came from behind her desk to see. "Perfect," she said, taking the box of wedding shoes in her hands and peeling back the tissue paper. "Oh. Perfect." Then to the almost groom: "You like?" He was short and stout with a grizzly beard. He nodded and shrugged at the same time.

The singles were women, mostly, and mostly older than my mom. There was one Marissa greeted as Eleanor, who wore a see-through blouse and a short stretch skirt and a pair of red lace leggings. Eleanor talked a million miles a minute—to Marissa, when Marissa was listening, to me when the phone rang—and she answered her own questions too. "Is this your first time? It must be your first time. Do you have a favorite dance? How could you? It's your first time. You've come to the right place, then, let me tell you, because Max, the owner, you know Max with the black hair? He won the U.S. National Professional American Nine Dance championship, and not only that, once he took the mambo at Florida. You ever see Max on TV? On one of those public television stations? You ever see him in the newspapers? Max, I'm telling you, is famous." I nodded, as if I expected nothing less. Eleanor wouldn't take her eyes off my shoes.

"What size do you wear?" she finally asked.

"Seven," I said.

"You young girls with your tiny feet—oh, what I wouldn't give."

I was rescued by another woman whom Eleanor called Annette, who was only slightly out of breath by the time Marissa buzzed her in. She had perfect legs, arctic hair. Her hazel eyes had dark, deep cores. She carried a notebook with her, where, I'd learn, she copied down her lesson steps. She carried, in addition, a pair of silver satin shoes.

"Annette!" Eleanor said.

"Hello, Eleanor."

"Are you working the mambo with Max today?"

"I believe we're working on the tango."

"This girl wears a size seven shoe," Eleanor said, by way of introduction, I guess.

"Rosie," Marissa said now from behind the desk. "The girl is Rosie."

"You'll love the dancing," Annette said, and she was one of those white-haired women who seem more young than old: the way she talked, the look in her eyes, the pure whiteness of her hair. I wanted to ask her something, anything. I thought: *She might have been Aideen if Aideen hadn't died, if Aideen were still with Granddad today.* But then Max was coming down the hall and calling out her name. He was saying good-bye to Teenie, blowing her a kiss, smiling. He had little beads of sweat on his forehead, but he didn't seem the least bit tired.

"Annette," he said, kissing her on the

cheek. He leaned down toward Annette's side of the couch and held out his arm. She stood and opened one elbow like a wing. They turned and, loop-armed, walked down the hall.

"I'm taking with Peter today," Eleanor explained as the two went off.

"Oh," I said. "Peter."

"Canadian," she said. "And superb. And boy, does he know the smooths."

I nodded again, having nothing to say. I didn't know what a smooth was.

Marissa had disappeared; she had vanished from the desk somehow. Eleanor had had enough of me. Sighing loudly, she crossed her legs and reached for something on a nearby table. I did as she did, sorted through the printed stuff until I found a book titled *Dance*. It was heavy and thick, a book of photographs and captions, and when I pulled it down onto my lap, it opened to a page titled "Rumba," to a map of Cuba, to pictures of dancers in skintight sparkle. "Rumba is a bridge to the past," I read. "To African desire and Cuban courtship. The rumba is primal." I stopped reading and looked again at the pictures. Skin and glitter. Hips. I turned the pages. I flipped back.

"The Argentine tango spirals up from hearsay and legend," I read, between photos of men and women dressed in severest black and bloodiest red, photos of men and women tight and close. "It comes from slang and intrigue, from the habañera rhythm that had drifted out from the ports of Havana toward Argentina. From the iniquitous Barrio de las Ranas of nineteenth-century Buenos Aires. From the rising tide of European immigrants and pampas cowboys, from native impulses and European influences, from the primitive and the lyric, from joy and melancholy. Tango is barrel organs and guitars, opera traditions and street singers." I tried to understand what any of this meant. I tried to fathom the fox-trot of New

York City and the waltz of the Hapsburg court, the cha-cha of Cuba, the samba of Brazil. I couldn't get enough of the pictures or the words. I could not stop checking the clock. Some new dancers buzzed in and strapped on their shoes. Some dancers left. I kept reading.

"Rosie Keith?" Finally I heard my name and looked up, and it was Max, Max releasing Annette from his arm, Max bowing in my direction. "Your first lesson?" he said, opening his elbow for me.

"My first," I said, and let him help me up. I hooked my arm in his in my best Annette style. I took the long way down the hall.

SIXTEEN

HE ASKED ME TO walk across the floor, just a regular walk; I did. He said to walk backward, and because he asked me to, I did, self-conscious in tall shoes. Do you know how when someone is looking at you and very exclusively at you, you feel put together wrong? That, right then, was me.

Max was—best guess—early thirties. He wore his hair short and slicked back, and up the long pole of one of his forearms were little twines of leather. His jeans were dragging-on-the-floor black jeans. His shoes poked out from his jeans. "Chin up, back straight, " Max told me, and then: "Put your heart toward my heart. Yes. Right. Now hold this frame and dance."

He stepped forward, and I slid back. He stepped to the side and took me with him. He stepped back and I stepped forward, and then we did it again. "The waltz," he said, as if he'd just introduced me to his aunt. "And the count is three-quarter time." I could feel the muscles of his arms beneath his shirt. They were Olympic-caliber muscles.

It was three fifteen in the afternoon, and besides me and Max and a wedding couple there were Eleanor and Peter, who was tall with narrow hips. She was leaning her forehead lightly against his, an odd, nervous look on her face. "Turn the music off," I heard her say after she'd tried several moves, none of which had made her happy. "I don't know what I'm doing."

Peter said something about the bend in

her knee. Eleanor said she was feeling off-balance. The music kept playing, and they started again. They wound their way close, and I stepped back.

"Keep your focus on your own lesson," Max said. I blushed, and we box stepped and made yet another round of boxes. Max said I'd need about a pound of attitude. He said I'd have to come to think of music as my skin. But first, he said, there is posture and spine. There are the basic fundamentals, and we'd spend our time on that. I thought about Granddad down the street, maybe asleep. I thought about Leisha, and Nick, and Rocco, and my mom. I thought a lot about Mom.

We boxed again and then more, long enough for Max finally to take what he called my measure. There were little crumbs of green in his eyes, though his eyes were mostly dark, and he stood so straight, you'd have thought he carried some coin upon his head. Rubbing the bottom of his chin, he shook his head thoughtfully. Then he framed me up again with his arms, and I remembered a doll I had on a shelf at home, propped up in a metal wire stand. You can't actually look at someone who is standing so close, even if you want to, even though you know, when you tell Leisha about it whenever you tell Leisha about it, that she'll ask you everything.

Now Eleanor and Peter were splashing against each other like buckets of paint; something he must have said had turned her *can't* into a *can*. And now through the door that opened to the roof came Marissa, a puff of cigarette smoke trailing behind her. If she recognized me from two hours before, she didn't act as if she did, and now she cut across the floor and disappeared, and then I heard Max was counting. "One TWO three and one TWO three and one," he was saying, and I was trying to keep up, and just when I thought that maybe I could get the hang of that one step, he said that it was time to test my rumba.

"My rumba?" I said, wiping the sweat off my forehead with a gooey palm, and he said yes, the rumba, and he started counting, not with numbers but with words, *slow quick-quickslow*, *quickquickslow*, adding a *quicker* after *slow* before he stepped forward and I stepped back, and he stepped to the side and I went with him, and then he stepped back and I stepped forward and tried to remember whatever I'd just read.

"Think of weather," he said, "and geography," fitting one hand to the base of my neck and one onto my shoulder, to release me, he said, from myself. He bent down and wedged out my feet until they were pointing away from each other. "Compass needles," he said. "Think of that." He said to try to keep my torso still so that I could work the hips, the knees, the feet. "Count with me, Rosie. Slow quickquickslow, quickquick—"

"—slow," I said.

"Quickquick—"

I felt like a two-year-old. It was so much harder than I'd thought it would be. I'd been crazy, absolutely, to think I could learn to dance. I pulled back from him and caught my breath. "No one ever said," I said, "that dancing was so tough."

"No one's an instant dancer," he said.

"I just thought—"

"You're not supposed to think. You are supposed to dance. Think of yourself as a rag doll for now. Let me see what you can do." Max went to the sound booth to change the song. He returned and stood before me, still. Then, to the music that had started to play, he led me through a dance. "Show me your split," he said, and I did the lousiest one. "Put your arm across my shoulder here, and let me lift you as I spin." I felt my hair get hot and loose with curls, my waistband pull. I felt myself being carried across the floor. We were stopping; we were starting; we were spinning, stepping, stopping. We were small steps and tight steps and scallops and lines, and Max was thinking, and as he thought, the green parts of his eyes got bright. "All right," he said. "There's talent here. Definitely something to work with."

"I have to get really good really fast," I said.

"With dancing there's no rushing."

"I know," I said, and felt my face get hot. "But this has to do with my grandfather." We were walking down the hall now, my arm linked with his. There was a gorgeous girl my age out on the couch lobby, fixing her shoes, waiting for him to call her name. "It's a long story," I said, feeling weird again about my shoes. "But I can tell you next time."

"You'll have to practice when you're not here," he said. "And you'll have to take a lot of lessons."

"I will do both," I said.

"Dancing is expensive."

"I have money."

"Check the schedule with Marissa then," he said. "Sometimes the evenings are best."

SEVENTEEN

THE NEXT DAY started out hot and got much hotter. It began with the sound of crows and the buzz of a juicy housefly that I'd probably let in through the back door by mistake when I was inviting fireflies. Mom was home but not up, and I knew without getting out of my bed how she was lying in hers, her face toward the two old windows she'd have propped up with wide sticks. She'd told me once when I was little that she liked to smell the sky. Not the air but the sky; there was a difference, she said. The sky was what pushed down on us, and the air was what rose high. Sky had the smell of stars in it. Sky had the smell of the moon. I didn't believe then, and I don't believe now, that I've ever smelled the sky, even in spite of Nick Burkeman and even in spite of my mother.

Except for the crows and the fly, all was quiet. I lay in my bed on my back with my arms pretzeled behind my head, thinking about rumba and box steps, about Max and silver shoes, wishing my mother would push open my door, push her head through, say something, one thing that would make me feel safe again, that would make me trust her with my secret. How have you been? I wanted her to ask me. How's Granddad? I waited. I waited. Granddad has a nurse named Teresa, I would have told her, except that now she'd made me wait too long. Granddad's been playing Sammy Davis Jr. songs. Granddad's been talking about Grandmom. Granddad hardly eats, he's hardly thirsty. I've started dancing. I wanted to be asked what now I would not tell, because she wasn't up and she still had not gotten up, and I had already found out for sure that I was plenty old to take care of myself. I didn't need my mother. I just wanted her to come and find out about me, ask me for her sandals back, notice how I was changing. I wanted her to look and see me.

But she wouldn't and she didn't, and it got to be stupid, lying and waiting, so I started doing morning things. Took a shower. Brushed my teeth. Pumped on my mascara. Put my wet hair up in a plastic claw and tied on my sneakers. I was going straight to Sweet Loaves for breakfast, I'd decided. I had money to spend, and I loved those raisins fresh.

"Rosie?" I heard my name when I was halfway down the steps, coming from the kitchen, not the bedroom. She must have sneaked down while I was primping.

"What?" I stayed just where I was, took no step farther.

"Could you come here, Rosie? For a minute?"

"What for?"

"Please, Rosie. Don't make me yell. You know how I hate that."

I came down each step the way an old turtle would, scraping the bottoms of my sneakers against the navy-blue nubs of the treads and risers. Mom didn't tell me to hurry up, and I knew she wouldn't; she was, by virtue of her own vanishing act, losing her right to order me around. Finally I was down, and where I stood was navy blue, and where she stood was marigold colored. She was wearing her bunny rabbit robe, and her hair was ponytail high. In her hands she held a tea mug.

"I wanted to talk with you," she said.

"What for?" I asked, standing right where I was.

"Could you sit with me for a while?"

"Granddad's expecting me."

"This won't take long."

I didn't budge. "I can hear you from here."

"Rosie."

"I'm not planning on changing my mind about Mr. Paul, if that's what you're hoping," I said, coming a little, most reluctantly closer, leaning my hips against the kitchen opening.

"You don't have to like him, Rosie. But you do have to be polite."

"I don't see why."

"I want him to feel welcome here. I want—"

"He's married, Mom."

"I know what he is." Suddenly she looked minuscule sitting at the table with her fuzzy rabbit on. She'd pulled her knees up to her chin, and she still had both hands on the mug, and she was looking out the window, toward the stiff black socks on Mrs. Robertson's line, all marching in a row to nowhere. I wasn't going to talk about Mr. Paul. I decided right then that I wasn't.

"Did you know Granddad has a nurse?" I said.

"That's what I wanted to talk with you about."

"You knew?"

"Of course I knew, Rosie. I talk with Granddad's caseworker every day."

I stared at her so hard that she must have felt me looking through her, until finally she turned and stared back at me. "I thought you were mad at Granddad," I said, tying my arms up into such a big knot that nothing she could say next could hurt me, or surprise me, or throw me off my balance.

"That doesn't mean that I don't love him."

"If you loved him, you'd go and visit."

"I will."

"Yeah? When?"

"When I can, Rosie. When I can. You have to trust me."

"The nurse's name is Teresa," I said. "And she has a tattoo for a bracelet."

"Teresa has had to make a few changes at Granddad's house," my mother said, "which is what I wanted to tell you. Wanted you to know, Rosie, before you got there."

I felt my heart throwing itself around in my chest. I felt my tongue get all dry and sticky. "What do you mean?" I asked. "What are you talking about?" My voice was louder than my mother liked, but I couldn't keep it gentle.

"She's just making things easier on him, Rosie, is all."

"Like what things easier?"

"Like he needs a wheelchair—not all the time but sometimes. He needs his life all on one floor. He's getting weaker, honey. Teresa is there to help. She'll be there now around the clock, sleeping in an upstairs room."

My mother turned and looked back out the window. Kept her chin on the table of her knees and her hands wrapped tight around her mug, and I could feel that she loved Granddad, I could feel that it was true, but

I was also the kind of frightened that came out as anger, the kind of frightened that blamed her.

"Rosie, I'm sorry," my mother was saying, but I couldn't hear her anymore; I wouldn't. "Rosie—" but I was already running, flying, through the dining room, through the living room, through the front door. My sneakers slapped the sidewalk and the road and the turn in the road and made tunnel echoes, then, under the railroad tracks, made sneaker sounds beneath the House of Dance. I ran past every single store without stopping. I ran, and I heard the crows flapping behind me. I ran, and I was faster than any train. I ran, and I was calling out his name— *Granddad! Granddad!*—long before I was close enough for him to know that his true one granddaughter was on her way.

EIGHTEEN

TERESA MET ME at Granddad's side door, her tattooed wrist draped with a towel, her hair back and high in a clip. "Rosie," she said, blowing her Spanish straight through my name. "Rosie." Saying it twice, as if she were finishing my mother's sentence.

I was out of breath and sweaty. The crows were still so close that I felt their wing wind, the flying electric charges of all their quarreling, and my lungs were chewed up, my voice raspy. "Where is he?" I spat out, not meaning to spit, not really.

"Waiting for you," Teresa said. "Like always. But Rosie, listen to me, he—" I didn't give her time to finish, just motored forward on my hissy sneakers, past her, through the kitchen and around the corner, into the room of books and brown, leaving the squawking crows behind. The couch was gone. A La-Z-Boy too. In their place were a bed and a wheelchair in a little half circle, facing the window. Half the bed was propped up, to make a chair. Thin silver railings ran along the sides. Granddad was wearing his regular khakis and a white, short-sleeved shirt that had no collar and no buttons. He had no blanket, was hooked to no machines, but he sat behind the silver railings, a magazine low in his lap. The place smelled like chemical lemons. The sun was smashed against the window glass, pressing noisily through.

"Just the person I was looking for," Granddad said when he saw me, folding a page down in his magazine and setting the whole thing aside. Slowly. "Vietnam and Cambodia along the Mekong River."

I looked around the room, and there was Riot. There was the basket of In Trusts, the basket of D.L., no basket of Toss. On the floor was the Sansui, and beside that the record stash. Not everything had changed. A hot slick of sweat took the short road from the indent of my neck to the indent of my navel, leaving a stripe of dark on my lavender T-shirt. Teresa was standing against the far wall. I lifted my eyes, at last, to Granddad's.

"Hello," he said, because I hadn't.

"Hello," I said.

"Good to see you," he said. "Rosie." Putting my name out into the silence.

I didn't answer. I heard Teresa, who must have gone back into the kitchen. Teresa picking up dishes, rinsing things. The sound of spraying water. The tinkle of glass against glass. Teresa now humming.

"Cat must have your tongue," Granddad said.

"Cat's got her own tongue," I mumbled, looking now at Riot, who had begun to give herself a fancy spa treatment. Her two back legs were stuck out at a ninety-degree angle. Her two front paws dabbed this way and that, maintaining her balance. "Where did you get Riot, anyway?" I asked finally, for the sake of saying something.

"Your mom gave her to me," he said, "when your grandmother passed. She was the runt of a litter. Needed some taking care of."

"Mom showed up with a cat one day?"

"Cat in a basket," he said. "If I remember. Your mother was pregnant with you at the time, so I guess that means you showed up too. She said, 'We'll both have our things now to be taking care of.' She said taking care was a cure, I remember." His eyes got misty at the end of his tale.

"Makes Riot a pretty old cat," I said, to distract him.

Riot went on bathing, oblivious. We watched her antics as if she were some kind of show, I standing with my arms tied tightly across my chest, Granddad in his metal bed, his face so pale in the shaft of sun that had worked its way inside. Teresa had turned the water off. There was stillness now on her side of the wall. Stillness everywhere.

"You got a new bed," I said.

"Feel like a Jetson," he said.

"It shines," I told him, because who knows what a Jetson is, "when the sun hits it."

"Yes, and there's quite a bit of sun."

"Next time I'm bringing shades," I said.

"I'm not going to stop you." Granddad said that part with a smile, and that felt good—warm in the way that warm is good— and suddenly that was all I wanted: to make my granddad happy again, to stop feeling so frightened and angry about his getting sicker.

Taking care is a cure, my mother had said. Back when she was smart.

"I see the old Sansui hasn't been budged," I said.

"After all you did to fix it up, Teresa and I weren't going to risk it."

"You in the mood for music?"

"Music would be fine."

"Anything in particular?"

"How about my old friend Ella?" He waved his hand toward the stack of records. I crossed the floor and started sorting.

"She have a last name?" I asked.

"Fitzgerald," he said.

"A rapper, right?" I asked him. I turned and saw him shake his head.

"She came from nothing to become something," he said. "A schoolgirl dreaming of becoming a dancer who became a singer almost by accident. Aideen adored her. I'd come home from the refinery, and I'd find her here, in this room, the furniture all shoved aside and Fitzgerald on the radio, live from Birdland or the Apollo or someplace. Aideen would be dancing with the moon. Whole moon or quarter. Never mattered. She'd have the music dialed up so loud that she wouldn't have heard me come in. I'd stand where Teresa is standing, watching."

Teresa, I remembered, and turned and saw that some runaway hair had fallen down into her face. She must have slipped back into the room like a shadow, and she was doing nothing but standing there, out of sight, almost. "Didn't you want to dance too?" I asked Granddad.

"Watching was sweeter."

"Didn't she mind being spied upon?"

"Don't think she did." He got a funny look on his face, the kind that Mom used to get when a new sprout of basil would push out of the glass or the fireflies would light up a room.

"What kind of dancer was she?"

"Nothing was more sensational than Aideen when she was dancing," he said. I tried to picture this, but it was hard. I pictured the candy-haired dancer on skyscraper heels instead. Pictured a peony on a wrist. Pictured a man, young, and a woman, young, but no matter how hard I strained to imagine, I couldn't make the man in my imagination look like Granddad, couldn't imagine my grandmother from the old, fuzzy photographs.

Outside, two drivers were blowing their horns at each other and a train was sailing into the station. A conversation shuffled by. I waited. "Somewhere in there," he finally said, looking toward the stacked records," is the song 'How High the Moon.'"

"I'm on it," I told him, but it took me a while. It took me sifting through and sorting the faded album covers until I found not just Ella but the right Ella, the right track on the right piece of vinyl, though Granddad didn't mind, he said, listening to "Old Mother Hubbard" first, or "Flying Home" or "Back in Your Own Backyard." He didn't mind whatever picture of Ella I found on the covers either, the one with her looking up at someone past the camera, the one with her wearing a white feather hat, the one with some guy looking mesmerized in the background. Anything Ella was good by my granddad. Anything Ella that day.

Finally I found it—"How High the Moon"—pulled it from its cover, got the Sansui whirling, laid the record on, and put the needle down on the right track. Granddad closed his eyes to listen. Out of respect I closed mine, too. Ella was singing. She sang raspy and demanding, giving the song speed. She held some notes forever and chopped others into bits, turned syllables into a million words. She was hard to keep up with, my granddad's Ella Fitzgerald, but still his eyes were closed, and he was smiling, and

Riot's tail was going around; the little triangles of her ears were twitching. Then the needle came up, because the record was done, and I could hear the crows outside, as if they had been waiting around for me. I could look into Granddad's face and know that he was sleeping. I listened for some sound from Teresa in the kitchen, but I heard nothing.

There are one hundred million different ways of feeling you're alone, I once wrote in a paper for Mr. Marinari. There's the alone of no one home but you. There's the alone of losing friends. There's the alone of not fitting in with others. There's the alone of being unfathered. But then there's also the alone of a summer day, just after noon, when there's stillness all around and someone you love nearby, asleep. I sat where I was, didn't budge one inch, and watched my granddad dreaming.

"What did you do today?" my mom asked me when I got home under the wing wind of crows, when the sun was the only color in the sky, after I'd taken my lesson with Max, after I'd found no cool in the tunnel shadows. My sneakers had hissed, but in that hiss I heard the scat of Ella Fitzgerald. There was no sound of Mr. Paul, not coming from the kitchen, not coming from upstairs. My mom was home early, alone.

"Ella Fitzgerald," I called to her, because her voice came from her bedroom, and her bedroom door was closed.

"Ella what?" she called back. She opened the door now, came out to the upstairs landing, and stood looking down at me, a river of navy-blue carpet between us. Her black hair was half up in a ponytail, half streaming messily down. She was wearing an old cotton dress, not overalls, as if she'd never been to work at all. Her face was puffy.

"Fitzgerald," I answered, not moving up the stairs, but not moving out of sight either.

"The singer?"

"Yeah."

A funny expression crossed her face. "He's got the record player working?"

"I got the record player working."

"Well," she said after a pause, "you're really something."

I didn't want her asking more. I didn't want to have to explain about the bed with the guardrails, the chair with the wheels, the air with the smell of lemons, acids, bleach. I didn't want to have to say how tired he was or tell her what Teresa had told me when I was leaving, how much sadder sadness sounds in Spanish. I didn't want to admit that there might not be time for me to give Granddad the present I was planning. "You know what I learned today?" I asked.

"What's that?"

"That I kind of like Granddad's music."

"Well, that's a good thing. I guess."

"Of course it is."

"Me and him, Mom. Me and him. We're

family." You could have confused my mom for a kid, I swear. She looked that small, that fragile.

"How is he?" she asked.

"He sleeps a lot," I said.

"I was guessing he would.

"He doesn't complain."

"I'm glad for that."

I had one foot on the bottom step by now, was waiting for my mother to come down so I could go up. But she sank to the step, put her elbows on her knees, her face in her hands. I understood that something had shifted.

"It's getting hot," I said. "Isn't it?"

"Have you eaten?"

"I had stuff." I had climbed a couple of steps up by now, closer to her. There were dark traces of mascara raccooned beneath each eye, a little bruise on the lip that she'd been chewing.

"We've got more than saltines and peanut

butter in this house," she said. "I could make you something."

"I'm okay, Mom. Really."

"Just offering."

"Tired," I said. "Headed for bed."

"Night, Rosie."

"Night, Mom." I slipped past her on the step and then, a few seconds after, came my shadow. I stepped through my bedroom door, closed it behind me, walked to the windows to find the moon. It was round on its way to getting rounder, Ella Fitzgerald style.

I threw open the windows to hear the crows in their trees and the next train coming. I pushed my head out to hear the *swish swish thrum* from the House of Dance, the music that was spilling through the windows there, fizzing up between downfalling stardust, knocking hard at my heart. I remembered all of a sudden a time that felt like centuries before, when Dad had come up with one of his crazy Christmas schemes.

He'd started taking me to Miss Marie, the local seamstress, sometime just after Thanksgiving. He'd had her make me a dress of purple velvet with a broad white collar onto which she'd threaded hot pink flowers. He'd had her make me a purple hair band too. Then one day we took a snowy walk to Miss Marie's, and everything was ready. I'd peeled off my everyday clothes, down to my undershirt and panties. I'd stood in the back of that shop with my hands high in the air while Miss Marie pulled the dress into place. I'd waited until she had zippered me up, and then she'd fixed my hair, and then she'd spun me around and called my dad's name, and he came in to see.

"Do you like it?" he'd ask me.

I nodded.

"Do you think your mommy will?"

"Uh-huh."

"You'll wear it Christmas morning then," he said, "when I give Mommy her present."

I remember changing back into my regular clothes. I remember Miss Marie handing my father two long bags. One that was little and mine, with the velvet dress. One that was longer and wide and held inside my mother's brand-new white wool coat. She'd wanted a coat so badly that winter. Miss Marie had made her one.

"It's our secret," Dad had said, and that was such a happiness. That was us, before.

NINETEEN

A LONG TIME AGO, when I was eleven, there was a luscious maple rooted deep in my backyard. It was wider than tall, and some of its limbs were loose, but I liked that tree because I had learned from its branches how to save Nick's lost planes. I could fish the sturdy balsa woods out from a mess of leaves and make Nick smile. I could dig out parts of planes from the maple's squirrel-nest hollow. Whatever I'd find, I'd run it straight back to Nick's place, hollering the news: *Smash-faced propeller. Stump of a*

wing. Splintered fuselage. Crushed cockpit.

But Nick was even better on that tree than I. He would scuttle out to the maple's farthest, hardest parts, up toward the sky or out toward the place where the limbs got lacy thin. "Checking out the stratosphere," he'd say. A word that branded him smart. "Testing. Testing." Like he was some kind of pilot. He'd shimmy up and the tree would shiver. When he stayed up there too long, I'd go get him some lunch, ziplock bags of bologna rolled up to look like logs, squares of cheese, a tall sleeve of saltines. Then I'd climb into the part of the tree that I'd nicknamed The Nest and wait for Nick to tell me something, and once in a while he would, and once in a while I'd go on about my celebrity father.

Then one warmish afternoon, when I was outside doing nothing and Nick was who knows where, Mrs. Robertson's cat, Claw, got wild for some bird that had built its nest on a thin bough of the maple. The big lug had climbed up that tree but couldn't get himself down; talk about sissy. "A predicament" is what Mrs. Robertson called it when she stomped over across her yard to ours and stood beneath the branches, looking up. By then Claw was mewing up a storm that the whole world could hear, and he would not stop his crying. "Come on, cat," Mrs. Robertson stood there saying. "Nice boy, kitty, kitty." But Claw was having none of her. He bared his teeth and stared, as if everyone and everything but him were to be blamed.

"You know, Cloris," said my mother, who had come outside to see about the commotion, "Claw will come down on his own. Give him time."

But Mrs. Robertson was fretting, and Claw was stubborn. That cat kept himself stuck, and he was clearly getting hungry, braying instead of mewing now, screaming, you might have said. Mrs. Robertson's face was never very pretty. Now it was scribbled every which way with worry.

Finally there was nothing to do and Nick wasn't home and my mother, trying to fix things, said: "Rosie, I've seen you. You're a mighty fine tree climber. You can scoot on up and shake that branch and make old Claw come tumbling down." A frame of reference and a strategy that left Mrs. Robertson staggered.

"Your plan is to shake my cat from your tree?" she said, gasping between the words, from shock.

"Do you have a better plan?" my mother asked.

"No, I do not," Mrs. Robertson said. "But even so." She looked from the cat to my mother to me and back up the tree.

"I guess that settles it," my mother said. "I guess I will go get a blanket." She went off in her sundress and her red flip-flops back into the house. Mrs. Robertson and I stood there, not talking, just waiting. After a while my mom returned, carrying our worst old plaid rag blanket, all folded up in a square.

"You and I will stand on either side of this," she said to Mrs. Robertson, snapping the thing out of its creases to its full size. "We'll catch the poor thing when he falls."

"Claw is not a circus cat," Mrs. Robertson said.

"He's a stuck cat," my mother replied. "We'll do what we can."

"I don't know," said Mrs. Robertson grimly, taking her side of the rag and pacing backward from my mother. "I sure don't like it."

"Neither do I," my mother said, her part of the rag in hand now. "He may be your cat, but this is my tree and also my blanket."

"Some blanket."

The maple was mature and secure in the ground. Its branches were messy over the lawn. When I stretched tall, I could grip my one hand around the lowest branch. When I pulled up, I could reach the next branch after that. That day I kicked off my shoes and took the slightest running start, to make my very best official tree-climbing-with-a-grown-up-audience debut. The branch was smooth and slippery to my touch, but my feet were off the ground.

I climbed. It was a nice-enough day. I got close but not too close to old cantankerous Claw. "Just shake the branch, Rosie," Mrs. Robertson called up from the ground. "You can do it from where you are." But as a matter of fact, I couldn't, because the klutz had got himself perched just out of reach. I had to go forward if I wanted to shake the thing free, but to get closer, I'd be in Nick territory. I let my right hand go, and I stretched, but no, I could not scrabble myself any closer. I tried again, got all trembly inside, hoped that I didn't show it. I glanced down toward the ground and caught Mrs. Robertson staring straight at me, her eyes like seeds, hard and tiny. I peeked and saw my mother, her eyes wider than normal, which made them rather basketball sized. The rag of a blanket they held between them was turquoise green and Santa red, little stripes running in all directions. The rag was stained and soggy, but it would have done, if only Claw would have jumped or lunged, if only I could have persuaded him to.

"Come on, kitty," Mrs. Robertson was saying. "Nothing to be afraid of. Jump."

"Don't be a scaredy-cat," my mother said, and started giggling.

"A nicer blanket would have helped," Mrs. Robertson said. "What kind of right-thinking cat would want to jump into this?"

"What kind of right-thinking cat—?" my mother started to say, then changed her mind, and I could hear all this, and I remember all this, but I remember thinking too that I wasn't going to be defeated by a one-eyed, overweight cat. That I was going to reach that high branch and jiggle the loser free, for all time and for the record. I shifted my position. Changed my hold on things. Strained my way toward Claw's hideout branch, and finally I could reach it, finally I was there, and I was pumping it, and Claw was seesawing up and down, holding on for his precious portly life until he could hold on no more.

I watched that cat slip and slide like the slow-motion part of a movie, and finally he leaped from his stuck roost. I saw his over-coat of dark fur getting smaller. I saw my mother and my neighbor tighten their grip on the Santa rag. I heard my mother saying, "Special delivery."

Then I was falling too, falling and falling from Nick territory, falling down through the branches. I remember my mother saying, "Oh, my God. Oh. Help us. Oh, Rosie. Honey. I'm so sorry." I remember the whack of the ground, which might as well have been stone. I remember my mother scooping me up in her arms and the drive to the hospital in the back of Mrs. Robertson's old-lady car, my head safe in my mother's sundress lap, my arm swelling up into a sausage, the pain like the pain of a heart attack, I suppose, but down around the fingers. I was in and out of sleep in a clean vinyl room, and then I woke up for good from the anesthesia, and I was puking out my guts. I'd smashed my wrist in three separate places. I had scratches that made scars I still have. I was wrapped up in a cast by some doctor I don't remember from my fingertips up to my shoulder, and that cast, from the very first, was steamy hot.

In the weeks afterward Leisha visited me at home, drawing her name in bright purples and pinks on my cast, telling me secrets, as she worked, about the people where she lived, who were getting richer by the second and buying multiples of fancy cars. Rocco came with a bag of crushed peppermint patties to perform his best stand-up routines—new material, he told me, though some of it wasn't very good at all and some of it was old. For my troubles Mrs. Robertson knitted me a new pair of socks to match, she said, my cast, and for being his one and only granddaughter, my granddad came every morning around nine o'clock to show me whatever he had found on the walk between our houses: A stone. A feather. A four-leaf clover. A paper-back novel that someone had dropped. A folded-up five-dollar bill. "Life is full of sur-prises," he'd say, holding my hand, but not saying much more, lining up his finds across my sill and leaving within an hour or so.

And then there was Nick, who designed me a plane that he launched from my very own bedroom window. Who told me the names of the birds he was seeing. Who found, he said at the end of one day, his owl. Who sat so close, I swear I could have kissed him. Almost kissed him. Dreamed I did.

But it's my mom I remember best in the weeks after the fall, my mom, who was always there, nearby and close, softly humming some song. We weren't alone, neither one of us back then, because taking care really is the cure. Taking care and staying close, which somehow my mom had lately forgotten or lately forgotten to believe.

TWENTY

THINK OF MUSIC, Max was saying a few nights later, as a garment or a shell, as a kind of shelter. Think of choreography as story.

It was our tenth lesson together, and he was working me hard, because that was the only way, he'd said, that I'd have a speck of a single chance to bring the dance to Granddad. He'd told me stories of his black cat, Fosse, stories of his competitions, stories about other dancers who'd come and gone, brilliant or moody or dangerous, all of them leaving a trail. Now Max's eyes were on something I couldn't see, his ears tuned to music I couldn't hear. He was still testing my limits. I was dancing in his shadow, dancing beside him, rising and falling and holding and turning and keeping the frame and respecting the sensor and carrying myself like a queen— trying to. "Shift your weight," Max said. "On *one*," he said. "Arms up, up, up, and down."

I was falling out of balance. I was falling in with him. There was nothing I could do but to take it slow and listen.

"No, Rosie, look at your hands," he said. "And look at where your left arm is, and pay attention to the count. Again, Rosie. That's the only way. You have to do it again."

I tried. Max started laughing, shaking his head. "The waltz is glides and turns," he said. "The waltz is confidence."

"I can't," I said, smiling so that he wouldn't know I was desperate, so that he wouldn't start doubting me even though I had begun to doubt myself. We'd danced together two hours every day since the first lesson. The dance he'd crafted was nothing but simple fundamentals. It would last only a minute. Any doofus should have been able to dance it well, but I was getting nervous.

"It's your deadline," he said.

"I know," I said. "But still."

"Listen," he said, "it isn't hard. It's a lift; it's turns; it's shifting weight; it's a twinkle and a breakaway and a right-hand wrap and a spin."

"Tomorrow night," I said, "I'll be better. I promise. Tonight I'm . . . off, I guess." Max's next lesson was already there, doing mambo hips in front of the reflective glass. She was tiny, dressed in purple. Her name was Julia.

"Confidence, Rosie," Max said. He covered his heart with his hand. Blew me a kiss, which is just a dancer's kiss and doesn't mean a thing.

"Same time tomorrow," I told him, leaving the floor.

"Rosie at six," he said. "I remember."

"I'm getting nervous," I said, "about the show."

"Don't. Just let it happen."

In the lobby, where I went to change my shoes, I sat for a long time, perfectly still, trying to shed my dizziness. Behind the front desk Marissa sat working the books, her skin cool and dry despite the fact that her partner, William, had been in. He came down from New York two mornings a week. Took the train, walked up the stairs—and they took over. On the mornings Marissa and William danced, there was nobody else on the floor. Then he'd leave, and she'd become her regular self, or as regular as Marissa got, which was not very regular at all.

"I think I'm a bit of a disaster," I said, for we had gotten to know each other a little by then.

"It just takes time," she said, not looking up. She was the sort of woman, I was thinking, you could never miss in a crowd of thousands. She was the sort who left an impression. Everything that Marissa wore was fitted. The skin under her makeup glowed. But her beauty was also in the way that she sat and the way that she stood: still and straight but unpredictable too. You had to watch her to understand. You had to watch her move. That day she was wearing low-rise white jeans and a pale pink scoop-necked top. She had glued a single rhinestone near the corner of one eye.

"I'm almost out of time," I said.

She closed her book. She put her pencil down. She looked at me as if for the very first time. The hair around my face was flat and damp. My dress was ordinary. I'd danced the life out of my mother's shoes, and I felt the opposite of girlie. Marissa knew about my plan to throw a party for my grandfather. She knew, all of the House knew by now, the hope I was hanging on to, the goal I was fighting toward.

"You have time enough," she said. "What you need is the right equipment."

"Equipment?"

"Shoes," she said. "Size seven?" She pushed herself out of her chair and disappeared to a back room. I sat on the couch in my bare feet, too surprised to move. A few minutes later she was back, a drawstring bag dangling from one hand. She came and sat beside me. "I'm a seven too," she said, "which is how I remembered." She loosened the neck on the pouch and slipped one hand inside. "I wore them only once, at a Rising Star competition," she said, revealing a bright red satin shoe. "Let's see if they fit you." They were the prettiest shoes I had ever seen.

Leaning down toward my feet, Marissa slipped the first shoe on, then tightened the buckle. She handed the other one to me, and I slipped it on myself. "Stand up," she said, and I did. "These are your new dance shoes," she said. "You start to practice in them now, and by the time of your party you will feel like you are dancing in bare feet. But leave them with me in between the dancing. These shoes have very special soles. They'd be ruined by the streets."

She was upright now, her back perfectly straight, her eyelashes casting feathery shadows on her cheeks. The phone started to ring, and she shrugged and did not get it. "They'll call back if it's important," she said. She sat there beside me. Her thoughts seemed far away.

"How did you learn beauty?" I finally asked, which sounded so stupid the second I said it, but there the question was. She did not turn. She did not laugh. I reached down to unbuckle the red satin.

"You know," she said at last, "I was ten. I'd been dancing since I was six years old. In Moscow. In Warsaw. In Düsseldorf. My father drove a truck. I was my mother's only daughter. Dancing was my family's hope for me. I lived and traveled with my coach and my partner, who was ten, like me. I was sponsored by my country. I was too far away, most of those years, for my mother to come and see."

I pictured gray skies and bright costumes. Big ballrooms and skinny kids. I pictured Marissa with another color hair, pale brown perhaps, like her eyebrows.

"Between the dancing at the competitions I was alone," she continued. "I was going in and out of dressing rooms, watching the women at their mirrors, watching their faces change with color, trying to understand how they could turn themselves into any mood they wanted. Some of the dancers let me sit beside them. They let me play with their buckets of paint. I made experiments. I learned."

"And your mother never came?" I asked.

"Once," she said. "My last competition before I came here to the States."

"And what did she say when she saw you dance?"

"She said, 'Marissa, you're a dancer.'" Marissa's eyes were wet, her eyelashes heavy. She turned and took a long look at me. "Mothers are proud people, Rosie. And beauty begins with color."

"These are beautiful shoes," I said.

"You are your own kind of beauty."

TWENTY-ONE

"TELL ME," I said to Granddad the next day, "about the places you always wished you'd been."

"The places?"

I was sorting the books now, into Toss, D.L., and In Trust, and also a fourth pile, Library. There were stacks about my feet, and I'd asked Granddad for a basic strategy, but he'd said that if I started, I would know just what to do. "Books can get brittle" is all he'd said, and I took that to mean the old encyclopedias, published in 1962, since there had to have been new facts since then, even new ways of deciding what facts mean. "We're pulping the old encyclopedias," I'd said to Granddad, and he'd smiled, which was his new approach to laughing. I'd gotten myself a system for the novels, too: In Trust the ones that looked mashed with reading, Library for those that looked too clean to have ever been of interest, and D.L. for books I might have wanted myself, though I was having the worst time deciding.

But then I got fixed on the travel books, all the fairy-tale trivia of the 1960s, the prices of places that might not exist anymore. The stuff was ancient and out-of-date, but it was scruffy, too, with handling. Dots on maps circled with green pen. Writing in the margins in blue ink. Pages accordioned in.

So I said, "Tell me about the places," because Teresa was in the kitchen pulping apples into sauce and Riot was snoring softly in her basket, and because this part of my

Granddad's past was, like so much else, a mystery. I took the travel books to him and puzzled them out on the bare parts of his bed: Montreal next to Venice, below Barcelona, across from New York, one step down from Verona, sliding to Paris, finally Seville. Country by country, cracks up their spines.

"They still teach geography in school?" Granddad asked when he saw what I'd done. One by one, slowly, he reshuffled the books, restoring, as he said, the world's quite fragile order.

"So they're important?" I asked. "In Trustable?"

"They were Aideen's," he answered. "They were how she got around in her own imagination."

"The books took her places?"

"The books were how she traveled."

I looked at him funny. "Just by reading?" I said, when what I meant was "Just like you?"

"And by looking at the photos, too. The maps. And by telling me about it later, when I got home from work." He said all that; then he was quiet. I could hear Teresa metal-smushing red deliciouses in the kitchen, striking the cold, hard-sounding bowl with her tool. I could hear the water running. "Money was tight," Granddad said. "Plus I was cautious."

"So her telling you was like her being there?" I was just trying to understand.

"The closest she could come. The closest I allowed. Oh, Rosie," he said, "what regrets." He stopped talking, and I tried to picture my grandmother in that room at night, moonlight coming in, maybe music riding a tune beneath her words, and the words smoking up like places you could touch and smell and make memories from, because the words were all she had. Both of them would have been younger than my mother is now. The house would have been younger too. The streets outside. All of it younger, and they just dreaming, my grandmother mostly just dreaming, going from nowhere to somewhere in her own mind, because money was tight and Granddad was cautious. And because she died, now Granddad had regrets.

"I've never been anywhere but here," I said.

"Every day's for living in. That's my new say-so." He asked for the eyeglasses he kept on the sill, and after I helped him pinch them to his nose, I wedged in beside him on his bed behind those bars. Slowly he turned the pages of the book titled *Seville*, running the tip of a blister-colored finger over photos of cathedrals, shops, pig thighs hanging from restaurant hooks like caveman clubs, white horses in dark streets, red flowers bursting out of the tops of roofs, big nests in chimneys, and bulls. Some of the photos had gone blurry with time, and some pages had torn a bit, and one page was missing, hidden somewhere, maybe, inside another book.

He traded *Seville* for *Barcelona*, showed me buildings that looked as if they had been built with drips of sand, streets you could play pinball in, a wide and very blue sea. He said, "I'm trusting that you've heard of Picasso? They teach him still, in your fancy school?" And when I nodded and he was done with Barcelona, he decided on *Verona* and started down its streets, sat his blister finger on the steps of its amphitheater, tripped it past the ghost of Romeo, until Verona was enough for one day. He slipped the glasses from his nose. I placed them back on the sill, helped him with his pillow, scooted the books off the bed as he straightened his legs. He closed his eyes, but not before I said that his eyes were the color of the Barcelona sea.

"The mistake I made," he said, "was thinking there'd be time for places later. I was wrong about that. I was a nest-egg man, feeding the bank what money I made, leaving

Aideen to her dreams. Dreaming Aideen's dreams for her later, but by then it was too late."

"She had you," I said. "And Mom. And music. Even if she didn't have places." He had started sinking deeper into his pillow, and the sun through the window had pressed a square of white light to his face that made that part of him so see-through that I could see past his skin to the skinny red rivers that rode up and down his nose.

"Your mother's mad at me," he said. "I wish she weren't." The words came out in ghost whispers.

"Mom can be funky."

"I tried to tell her, after your father left, about time and what it does, about living and how you have to, but she kept hearing different. She thought that I was criticizing. She thought I could not understand."

"Granddad," I said, leaning in so close, because that's how hard it was becoming to hear him, "you're tired. You should sleep."

"Plenty of time for sleeping," he said. "Plenty of time for that." But his fingers around my fingers were finally breaking their grip.

"Wishing you sweet dreams," I told him, and kissed his forehead, and turned and gave Riot a you-behave look. I sat where I was with him for a very long time. Only after the sun had taken its mark from his face did I slip from the bed and drag the travel books over to the pile of In Trusts.

"He's sleeping," I told Teresa, rounding the corner.

"You're a good granddaughter," she said.

"I have an appointment," I told her.

"I know."

"But I'll be back."

"You always are," she said, with her swervy Spanish lilt. "He trusts you, Rosie. Loves you."

I stared at the floor. I couldn't look up.

Outside Granddad's house time was fast-forwarding. There were birds that weren't crows on the railroad lines, a skateboarder on the sidewalk, three cyclists on the street going side by side, making a backup in the right car lane. The closer I got to Pastrami's and Whiz Bang and Bloomer's, the more people there were in the way, the more moms with strollers and kids, the more window-shoppers and businesspeople in the bright sunlight, going fast, the better I could smell the cinnamon bread at Sweet Loaves, plumping the air with so much sugar that the air was a sugar high. I stopped for the doggerel at Harvey's Once Read, the scribble of blue ink on the already sun-faded page:

I rose today to pure gray skies
But then the weather changed
And on the clouds that drifted by
Were birds and colors strange.

I looked past the doggerel through the smudged glass door, and there was Harvey, behind his register, sitting on his stool. He had pushed his glasses up on his forehead and was holding a book very close up to his eyes. The hair that he still had on either side of his head was all gray fuzz grown patchy. There were a couple of regulars at the Best in Store table, where Harvey always put his finds. I poked my head through the door and the chime rang. I waited for Harvey to glance up and see me.

"Nice doggerel," I said.

He did a half bow on his stool.

"It's your best one yet," I said. "I like the 'colors strange.'"

He smiled, and then I got on with my day. Someone had just pushed open the House of Dance windows. I looked up and caught a glimpse of Max and Annette, thought I saw Marissa. People were pushing in both directions. I walked on until I reached the awning that said Bloomer's. This was a place I'd only ever gone with Dad. It was dark, as it always was inside, except for way back on the other side of the store, where a bright light shone over a counter and workspace and the proprietor known as Annie Pearl. She was mostly gray with some blond still in her hair. She was wide and wore a gaping apron.

In the store itself there was hardly any walking room. Cut flowers were crammed into buckets and pails, they were leaning out of crates and vases, they had their blossoms caught in nets or were already past budding, and they smelled like the colors they were, like tangerine and grape and vanilla and lemon. I remembered coming once into the shop on my father's shoulders and looking down while he gathered a bouquet. I remember his saying, "Peonies, only peonies," and taking each one in the store—the white with the yellow center, the mango that was mango through and through, the burgundy—all just for Mom. "We'll tell her that we love her just because."

But today wasn't a just-because day. It was a because day, a living-in day, a planning-the-party-that-was-coming-soon day. "Hello, Annie Pearl," I called from the front of the store.

Annie Pearl looked up and squinted. "That you, Rosie Keith? All grown up, you are."

"It's me," I said. "How have you been?"

"It's our busy season," she said, gesturing toward the floor. "And we've got lucky with good stock. What can I do for you?"

"I'm planning my granddad a party." I just came out and said it. Wove my way between all the flowers to get closer to her counter.

"Are you now?" She smiled.

"I am."

"And what will you be needing?"

"I don't know much about the names of flowers," I said. "I just know that I want color."

"We're good at color."

"I'd rather have a few great flowers than a bunch of little ones. I know that, too." Annie Pearl took notes on a pad that had been sitting on her counter. "And I don't really care how much it costs, except if it goes past three hundred dollars."

"You win the lottery, did you?"

"In a fashion," I said.

She raised one eyebrow. "Your mother know about this?" she asked.

"She will soon enough," I said. I took out an envelope of twenties.

"I'm not going to want any of that," she said, batting my dollars away, my proof of my independent wealth, "until I've got your flowers."

I told her the date. She made more notes. I looked around the store and pointed at flowers that seemed special.

"Rosie," Annie Pearl said when I was leaving, "I got extra dahlias in." I turned to see her pointing to a bucket of broad-faced flowers, some of which were orange, some purple. "Do me a favor and take a couple with you. I hate to see them go to waste." She went back to work on that notepad of hers, made another couple of notes.

"You want me to take these?" I called back. "For free?"

"For the sake of the sunshine," she said. "For the sake of making the most of the very best of them." I wound my way back to the dahlia bucket. I stooped down close and did what she had instructed me to do. I chose the very best. Two orange and one purple. I thanked her and walked out into the sunshine.

TWENTY-TWO

THE WINDOWS WERE open at the House of Dance. I could hear the music playing as I took the diagonal across the street, met Annette on the steps, she coming down and I going up. "Max is in one of his moods," she told me.

"Oh, no," I said, and we both laughed. Annette had agreed to dance for my grandfather. They were working, I knew, on a foxtrot. Max and I had agreed on a waltz. It was what I was best at, what I could learn with the time that I had. "Hey, Annette," I said.

"Yes?"

"A dahlia for you." I handed her one of the three I had taken from the bucket of extras at Bloomer's.

"For me?" she said.

"Of course. For you."

"You're something else," she said. "And thank you."

Marissa buzzed me in. I laid the other two dahlias across her desk, then joined Eleanor on the couch. She'd just finished up with Peter; she could use a drink, she said: "And I'm not talking about lemonade, either." She flopped backward on the couch. She had one dance shoe on and one off. She had painted her toenails blue. She was wearing a long white skirt and a white lace tank, and she'd been working on her tan. "So how are the preparations, honey? Going well, I bet. Of course. You got everything you need right here in town. I wouldn't throw a party any-where else. And how about your dance—you got your dance all down pat? You know Max is a genius, Max makes the worst of us look good. Not that you're the worst, Rosie, I didn't mean that. I'm just saying don't you worry. You're in such good hands with Max."

Marissa had blown me a kiss for the dahlias by now and handed me the red satin shoes; she kept them behind the desk. "Gorgeous," Marissa said, about the dahlias.

"Was William here today?" I asked her.

"You just missed him," Eleanor answered, before Marissa could. "Oh, my God. Those two? Spectacular. You ever see their bolero? To die for, I'm telling you. And oh, by the way, what a terrific twosome of dahlias."

"William can come for the party," Marissa said, talking over Eleanor because that's the only way that anyone could talk when Eleanor was talking. "It's all confirmed."

"I don't even know how to thank him."

"He wants to do it. He doesn't need to be thanked."

"But will you tell him anyway for me? When you talk to him next, will you tell him?"

"Of course."

"Rosie?"

I turned, and there was Max, halfway down the hall with his arm winged out. I finished putting on my shoes and hurried off toward him. "Time is of the essence," he said.

"I'm sorry."

We began to dance the waltz as Max had designed it. I had my head pressed back, my posture as right as I could make it. I had this thought in my head that I could finally make my granddad proud, raise up in him the memories of something sweet and good. But then Max broke our hold and stepped back and said, "Now I want to see if you can count it out for me. I want to know what you know on your own."

"By myself?" I said.

"By yourself," he said.

Annette, I thought, wasn't kidding.

I felt silly all alone out there on the floor, with Max leaning against a windowsill while I boxed and whirled. But he was the boss, the nine-dance champion, and all I could do was slim the dance down to what I could actually do on my own.

"Okay," he said at last. "Okay. You're doing a lot of things right. You can do more, though; you can do better. I have a few ideas." He danced with his own reflection while I watched. He traced out choices. "I know what it is," he'd say to himself. Then: "No, no, no. It'll be this." I imagined him imagining the dance with a true partner, with an Annette or a Marissa, with the blonde whose name was Yvonne. I thought of how tiring it must be to dance at my beginner level.

"Okay," Max said, pulling me into a hold, "so we were here, and now," he said, elevating my left arm and placing my right hand on his shoulder, "we're here. And now you're walking while I turn, and now you're running—faster, faster—and now you're slowing, to a walk. Now you're planting your left foot, you're stepping out with your right, shifting your weight." I had no idea what he was talking about. He made me do it again. It was like running into the wind.

"Your hands are not in the right place," he said. "And your left arm is supposed to be back. And your count is off. So we'll do it again. Come on."

"Is this really necessary?" I said.

"If you want to be good, it is."

We did the whole thing again, and my head felt slung against itself. There were three of me in the mirror and four of Max in the room, and he was laughing, shaking his head. "We're going to have to do that again," he said. "Rosie." As if he had to remind me who I was.

"I think I'm going to get sick," I said.

"Try it again," Max said, and I said, "I

can't." He looked at me as if he hadn't heard me right. I said, "No. Really. I can't," and now his next lesson, Julia, was already there, practicing her mamba at the room's other end. She was the protégée, the studio's young star. She had less to learn than I did.

"Tomorrow," I told Max, because I wasn't joking about getting sick, and because he might have been the boss, but I was the paying client.

"Tomorrow's your favorite word," he said.

"Tomorrow. I swear. Tomorrow."

"All right. Tomorrow then. Keep the moves inside your head, so you can think them through your body."

TWENTY-THREE

"EVERY DAY'S FOR living in." That was what Granddad had said. Walking home now, after dance, I felt like rubber that had been left out in the sun, globby and dizzy and so not pretty, but happy too because I really was learning to dance. I really was going to give my granddad all that I could give of color.

I was through the tunnel now and back around to the street on which I lived, and all of a sudden I was thinking about Nick and that one sweet time that we had gone off in search of something big, taken what we wanted, gotten all caught up with time, had ourselves a verifiable adventure. We were thirteen. We'd escaped, when no one was looking, the Tuesday of our Easter break. We had run off to the station and boarded a train, telling no one, not even Leisha, where we were headed. An exhibition of old model planes had come to the city's science institute. Nick had seen the ad in the paper. I was his accomplice.

The train had been crowded, the morning rush. It was April, but I was wearing a skirt and sandals anyway, hoping Nick would notice, and Nick had his khakis on, out of respect, he had said, for airplanes. We were tight together in the commuter train, and his legs were long, his shoulders wide. He was looking straight ahead, not saying much, because he hardly did, and because he was excited, maybe, and then, when he turned to look at me, it seemed his eyes were made of sky. Every day's for living in, and that day, sure as the sun came up, was altogether Nick's.

There was a girl and a mother in the seat ahead of us, and the girl—maybe she was three—was wild. She'd be standing up, then kicking her legs out straight, like an acrobat in free fall. Every time she plopped down, the seat went squish, and she would let out a hiccup and laugh. When she grew tired of jumping, she banged at her mother for attention, who did precisely not one thing. Plain didn't move. I looked at Nick. Nick looked at me. The sky still in his eyes.

"Some mother," I said.

"Asleep," he said. "I guess."

"Who could sleep through that much racket?"

Nick shrugged. He looked at me, then past me at the world that was rushing by: garbage cans in backyards, dogs behind trees, little backyard sheds with metal roofs, inflatable swimming pool, crushed flat. "Can't believe we're doing this," he said.

"I can," I said. "Why wouldn't we?" Because we never had, that was the answer, but Nick didn't say it.

The girl in the seat ahead was bored, slapping at her mother's arm and getting nothing. Kicking at the back of the seat before her, until a shined apple of a head from across the aisle asked her to pipe down, please. It was when she turned around to see behind her that she fell at once for Nick. "Hello," she said, and Nick looked up, and then she saw his eyes.

"Wanna hear me sing?" the girl asked.

"Sing?" Nick repeated.

"Okay," she said, standing straighter, and Nick, looking at her as if he'd for the first time seen her, got this funny expression on his face. "I'm a real good singer," the girl said, and she was standing all the way up now, facing backward, facing Nick, planting both feet on the seat and starting in on some song. It was no song I'd ever heard, but it had rhythm and she held the tune, and now the girl was clapping to keep up with herself and smiling white through seashell teeth. All the little braids that spiraled out from her head closed up tight in kitten-shaped plastic clips, and she had some kind of jumper on and a shirt with a tiny collar. You couldn't not see how she was saying "Dance with me," and somebody from across the aisle saw it too, joined in with a little nodding rhythm, and now the girl, having found herself a bigger audience, grew even taller in her seat and sang a little louder with her frothy voice. All this while her mother slept, her head slammed against the window of the train, her breath hawing heavily.

The world outside the train kept rushing by. In the seat my thigh was pushing up against Nick's thigh; and if at first, while the girl was starting her song, Nick didn't move one inch, just stared, now I saw the big boots on his big feet slide, a sort of shuffle to the right, a shuffle to the left, in time to the little girl's song. Nick dancing. Nick taking the rhythm in, putting the rhythm out, and all the years I'd known Nick, had lived next door to Nick, lain flat on a roof beside Nick, chased his homemade planes, I hadn't known that Nick had dance in the bottoms of his boots.

The girl reached the end of her song, blew the last word out of her little-girl cheeks, jumped up, then came down in her seat, popped back up, and said, "Don't worry, I got another." Now she was off again into some new tune, and there were more on the train helping her keep up her beat: commuters with briefcases, mothers with kids, other people like Nick and me, but not shiny apple head. Nick's boots were going left-right-left-right-left-right, and my right sandal foot was going with his left black boot, because we were sitting thigh to thigh, because this was Nick's day, and Nick had decided to dance.

"I got something," the little girl said, now that she had us all in the palm of her tiny hand, and Nick said, "What's that?" and the girl said, "I got these," and Nick said, "What these is it that you got?"

"These," the little girl said—said to Nick because he was the one she liked the most, because she wanted to give her special something to him. Before we could guess what she meant, she was yanking at the plastic clips in her hair, the kitten barrettes, yellow and red, that piled up quickly in her hands. She pulled at her hair, but her braids stayed put.

"She shouldn't do that," I said.

But Nick said nothing.

"Her mother's going to freak."

"Her mother's sleeping."

"I got these for you," the girl said. "For you, for you, for you," she said, jumping herself silly. She tossed her fistful of barrettes over the seat back, at Nick. They went up like fireworks and down like rain, landing in his lap. She screamed, it was so funny.

"I got more," the girl said, putting her hands back up to her braided hair, snatching another kitten free. But now her mother finally woke herself up from whatever dream had made her dead, and I could see, but barely, her face through the crack between the seats: her sleep-mussed hair, her anger.

"Honey, I told you," the mother said, shifting in her seat, changing the fractions of the face that I could see. "I told you, you take those barrettes out, you're not getting any more, you listen? I told you to leave your hair alone!"

"That's my friend," the girl said, pointing to Nick.

"Nobody here's your friend," said the mother, not turning. "Now you sit down and say you're sorry. You sit down. Be good."

"It's all right," Nick said, leaning forward.

"She's a performer."

"She's a diva is what she is," the mother answered. "A circus clown. Can't sit, this child. Can't sit. I told her." Then to the girl: "No more." The girl was disappearing. Her face bobbing down and then up, then bobbing down. I could hear only her whimper, her crying.

Through the windows of the train the landscape was turning to industrial waste, small scraps of trees, birds on a wire. The empty plastic trash bags that got caught in the wind looked like green and white ghosts, floating. There was a dog on a hill. There was the start of the city. A building built of blue-green glass like a ship berthed in the sun. The conductor was announcing Philadelphia. People were shuffling, collecting things, and the girl and her song were all forgotten, but still there was that shower of barrettes, and when I looked back at Nick, I saw how he was stringing them together—red to yellow to yellow to red, a bracelet of hair-clip kittens.

"Nice," I said, but Nick said nothing, and by the time the train stopped in Philadelphia, Nick stood to let me slip on past. "See you around," I heard him say behind me, and when I turned, I saw him reach to give the girl her barrettes back. She was fast asleep, curled up against her mother, who was herself asleep again. There were people behind Nick and me, pressing to get out. There was the morning rush.

"Liked your songs," Nick told the girl, laying the barrette bracelet down on her lap.

"Me too," I said, now walking forward, ahead of the crushing crowd. I could feel Nick close behind me, in the aisle. I could feel him behind me as we stepped out. It wasn't far to the institute after that. Down the escalator, through the station, across an old bridge over a brown river past a black tower, through a wind blast. We turned a corner, walking side by side. We took the institute's wide white steps. We paid with birthday money, each of us. We lived that day, like Granddad said.

TWENTY-FOUR

THE NEXT DAY AT Granddad's Teresa met me at the door. "He's had a little setback," she said. "I've got him sleeping."

I felt my heart jitter up inside the narrow knob of my throat, my hands go clammy. "I'm coming in," I said. And then, when she didn't move: "Aren't I?"

She looked at me so carefully that I wondered what she saw: my tangled hair all scrunchied back, my T-shirt loose, my long shorts baggy. "He needs his rest," she said. She was wearing a buttercup-colored T-shirt and a gauzy skirt, brown sandals without much of a heel. I crossed my arms in a most outright duplication of hers.

"I'm good at quiet," I said.

"I know you are, but Rosie—" *Rosie.* My name, with the Spanish curlicue *R*, my name spoken as a warning.

"I'm family," I told her. *"Family."* One of the biggest words in any language.

She looked at me for a long time before she finally unknotted her arms. I was past her in a second, around the corner of the kitchen and right there, quiet, next to him, in his prison bed, beside the tangle of wires of a machine—it hadn't been there before—that was needling something into his veins.

"What is this?" I demanded of Teresa, who'd followed me and was now right there beside me.

"I was trying to tell you."

"You didn't tell me *this*," I said, thrusting my chin toward the IV.

"He needs it. For the pain. For fluids, Rosie."

"Yeah. Well. He hasn't said anything to *me* about pain." My heart was a live frog in my throat. The heat of the day was getting stuck behind my eyes. I was mad again, but mad wasn't right. And Teresa wasn't wrong. I was.

"We should talk, Rosie," she said, "the two of us."

"I'm not," I said, "going to." Two words only in each long breath.

"Today we're managing the pain, yes? We're managing the pain and the fluids. Today." Every one of her words playing like music, even the serious ones.

"It sucks," I said, not taking my eyes for one second off Granddad. "Totally."

"Yes, sucks," she said. "I know it sucks. But he'll want you here where you are when he wakes up. And he won't want you mad."

"I wasn't planning on going anywhere," I told her, flopping down so hard in the mean-

202

looking wheelchair that I probably bruised my butt.

"Me also," she said, taking the remaining La-Z-Boy chair, scaring Riot out of a doze. "Nowhere."

"It's me *either*," I said, "in my language." I sat looking at Granddad. She sat looking at me. The room was dull brown and white sheets, bed bars and wheelchair metal. I said, "If you want to tell someone about it, tell Riot."

It was like Mom had said: Multiple myeloma is apocalypse business. Too much calcium swimming around in the blood, bungling the kidneys. Too many plasma cells in the marrow messing with the immune system. Things getting stuck, things drying up, things dying. Hypercalcemia. Pneumonia. Infections. It's the end-of-the-line stuff for multiple myeloma, the way people die when they're that sick. Granddad was doing pretty well, considering. But still, Teresa said. Still. Things were changing. He was changing. I had to be prepared. While Teresa talked, Riot walked all around. She jumped from the floor to my knee to the floor. She jumped to the windowsill. She stared at the people walking by outside, the people who couldn't see us where we were, in a cave of sickness, running out of time.

"Where does he hurt right now?" I asked, for Riot's sake.

"Everywhere he's aching," Teresa told the cat, who swiped just then at something with her monster-sized pipe-cleaner tail, then bent around on herself and nibbled at a hind leg. When Granddad sighed in his sleep, when he shifted just a little in his sheets, Riot's ears went out like two antennae, a direct tilt toward his bed. She was better than a guard dog. She knew Granddad the best.

"Why does he hardly eat anymore?" For the sake of that cat I asked.

"Too much to ask of the kidneys. And the food—it doesn't taste so good; it's more like work."

"What are you doing for my granddad? What *can* you do?" *My* granddad, I'd said. *Mine.* Because so what if he belonged to Riot? He also belonged to me.

"Make him comfortable. Bring him what he wants." She was turning a strand of hair around one finger. When she stopped, a curl was there. I watched her. I wondered what would make her care so much about an old man she'd only just met, how much sickness she had seen, and how much dying.

"He wants me to put things In Trust, is what he really wants," I said. "I know that for a fact."

"No doubting, Rosie." She chose another ribbon of hair and twined it around.

"And all I've gotten to so far is the books and the things in between the books and the songs. And that's not much."

"A lot already."

"Not enough."

I felt the heat of the day packing back in behind my eyes. I watched Riot leap from the windowsill, like water falling down. "You don't know how hard it is," I told her. "Deciding. What to keep and what to throw away." I didn't want to cry. I hadn't meant to. But all of a sudden I was drying my cheeks with my hands; my hands were wet. Riot had left the floor where she'd landed and leaped right back up to my lap. She was padding my knees, softening them for a nap. I put one of my wet hands on the silk of her head until she finally quieted down.

"A hard job, deciding," Teresa said.

"And it's not like my mother has come around to help." I felt another warm leak down my face. I didn't dry it.

"Everything in its own time, Rosie."

"Why are you here?" I asked Teresa, after I'd settled myself.

She thought for a moment. "To make a difference." She had two long curls hanging beside her face. She was working on a third.

"No, here. In the United States. Why are you here and not wherever you're from, doing this?"

"Ah," she said. "Andalucía, you mean."

"White horses. Red flowers. Black bulls." Lifted straight from my grandmother's travelogues, which I'd tucked safely away In Trust.

"Well. That is a story."

"Granddad's asleep," I said, knocking away the last of the tears. "And so is Riot." The Maine coon was purring like a revving car.

"I guess we have time then to tell."

I scrunched around in the thin-seated wheelchair. I looked at the room, dull brown and sheet white except where the hospital metal caught little pricks of sun. I wasn't leaving until Granddad woke, and I didn't want to sit with my thoughts.

TWENTY-FIVE

"GO AHEAD," I said, and Teresa began with color. Color in the skies, color in the earth, color in the marketplaces, where she would go, she told me, as a little girl to help choose the hard green tomatoes and the not precisely ripe yet plums and the Manchego cheese that was more than three months old and also the youngest partridge, the pinkest pork, the white-bellied sea bass, the red mullet. But the brightest colors, Teresa said, were the flamenco colors, flamenco being more than a dance, more of an invention performed in black boots and dresses that looked like animals no regular body would for one minute trust. Flamenco was back there, back then. It was home.

Teresa's father had been a banker. Her mother had been a beauty. There had been a cook named Stella and a garden of yarrow, aster, chive, marigold, and in that garden there'd been butterflies—wings, Teresa said, like so many stained glass windows. There had been places to sit in the garden. There had been birds.

But what happened to Teresa when she was ten was the reason she had come to be in my country, in my grandfather's house at the time of his dying. She had been sitting with her mother on the couch one day. She had been sitting, looking outside at the flowers. Both of them wearing silky white pajamas, both of them just resting.

Then Teresa's mother had gone upstairs and, after something more than the usual time, had not returned. There was, Teresa said, something wrong all of a sudden blowing through the house, and now she was up off the couch and running across the floor and through the kitchen and up the curving marble steps of that big white house, calling for her mother. And then there she was, her mother on her back, on the black-flecked marble of the bathroom floor. Teresa had turned the water off in the shower stall and cried out for help until Stella had heard, but there was nothing for it. Her mother had been alive. Next, her mother was gone. One thing, then the other.

After that, Teresa said, she would let no one touch her mother, no one. It was Teresa herself, ten years old, who buttoned her mother into her burial gown and tied her hair in a ribbon and powdered her eyelids with a lilac color and blew the dust from between her lashes. It was Teresa. Afterward there was only sadness in the house and her father working longer hours at the bank. Stella stopped making gazpacho, stopped peeling cloves of garlic, stopped putting the old bread in water to soak, stopped going to the market for clams. The garden grew knotty and cold. The butterflies went elsewhere. Teresa herself woke every morning thinking maybe she would go downstairs and find her mother, dressed in white.

"I'm glad you're here," I said when her story was done.

"There is time," she said. "Still. With your grandfather."

"I have been planning something," I said.

"What precisely is it?" she asked.

And I told her.

TWENTY-SIX

ON THE WAY-OPPOSITE end of the strip from where Granddad lived are the places people go to get things fixed. The shoe guy, quick with new soles. A strange wrinkled woman who won't say much but is purely brainy, people say, with messed-up jewelry and clogged-up clocks. It's where the town's big banks sit, and also the fast-serve burger joints and the three gas stations facing off on a single corner, one of them the station where Nick works with his dad in the summer, the two of them scurrying around like crabs on their backs, going face to belly with snagged autos.

The day after Teresa's stories, the morning after I had danced well, at last, with Max, and before I got to Granddad's, I went to see Miss Marie—swung up and around and beneath the tunnel, beneath the too-early-for-action House of Dance, and headed west, paralleling the train tracks until I got to where I was going. There was a thick bracelet of jingle bells pinned to the inside of Miss Marie's door, and when I walked in, that thing rang, a bizarrely winter song in summer. It wasn't long before Miss Marie appeared, broke through to the front of the store from the back, where she'd been working behind a pair of thick paisley curtains. Miss Marie was like a walking time capsule, stuck in back who knows when, with her dyed brown hair tied up high on her head with a little purple bow. She was wearing a white blouse with a pointy collar and a dark-purple pleated skirt—had on black tights and gray ballerina-style slippers. She looked precisely the way she had looked all those Christmases ago.

"Why, Rosie Keith, hello," she said, after she had squinted at me through her magnifying glasses. "Have you ever grown," she said, taking her glasses off and setting them aside. Not a question, so I didn't answer.

Her shop was long and narrow, like a coffee bar, which is what it was in the old days, my father had told me once, before she took it over. It had two pink chairs at one end, like dollhouse chairs, and a mirror straight between them, and on three round tables with scratched glass tops there were mounds and mounds of fabric samples. A bunch of magazines was flopped on the floor, some teal-green binders, and on the wall opposite the mirror and chairs was a poster of Princess Diana. If anything had changed since I had been there years before, I didn't see it. Even the tomato pincushion that Miss Marie wore on her wrist was the same; so was the little pair of silver scissors that hung from a ribbon like a necklace.

"Busy, Miss Marie?" I asked.

"Always," she said. "And always a pleasure to help you." She sized me up with her eyes, as if she were halfway toward making me some floaty, boy-eye-catching summer dress, and of course I stopped her right there.

"What I need," I said, "is a wheelchair cushion. Something to take the edge off the hard, thin plastic."

She frowned for a moment, a thousand pleats closing in around her eyes.

"Everything okay at home?" she asked.

Ha, I thought. *Don't even go there.* "It's for my granddad," I said. "He's not been well."

"I'm sorry to hear that." She looked at me hard, waiting for more, but I was here on a business call and wasn't about to explain about the apocalypse cancer—the calcium, the kidneys, the bones, the running short of time.

"It's a troll-ugly wheelchair," I said. "And

it's hard as stone to sit on. I was thinking of something soft and fancy."

Miss Marie brightened. "Tassels?" she asked. "Piping around the edges?"

"Something like that," I said. "Something fabulous. Gallant." I liked that word, *gallant*. I had seen it in one of Granddad's books.

"It won't have to cost much," she told me, touching the purple ribbon that was pulled so tight at the top of her funny, pointed head. "I've got fabric ends, won't even charge you for them."

"Money," I said, "is not an issue."

"Size?" she said.

"Got it." I pulled a crumpled piece of paper from the pocket of my shorts. I had measured the day before, with a twelve-inch ruler I had found in one of Granddad's kitchen drawers.

"You don't mess around," Miss Marie said, "do you?"

"Not when there's so little time, I don't." She put her glasses on now, to look at me again. I let her look as long as she had to.

"I'll make this a priority," she said after she'd satisfied herself.

"Thank you. And also?" Here I got shy and a little self-conscious, stumbling a bit.

"Ah," she said. "Something for you?" she asked.

"A dress," I said, searching for words. "Something special. Something pure and simple and soaked with color." She took out her measuring tape, and I lifted up my arms. She brought spools of things from the room behind her. She showed me pictures, patterns, threads. I asked if she worked fast.

"Fastest anywhere," she said. "Come back in three days, and you'll have a dress."

"Don't forget the wheelchair cushion," I said.

"Four days," she said.

The bright-red digitals on the bank read 84° F and 9:46 A.M. when the jingle bells rang me out of Miss Marie's. Early still in Granddad's world. Teresa would be wanting him to herself; that's how she'd put it. For baths, for medicines, for talking to. For whatever nurses do, their secrets.

Already the heat of the day was roofing over everything—the buildings, cars, and sidewalks, the people and the trains. The heat was there, and above the heat was the sky, and in between the heat and the sky a few birds flew. At the gas stations across the street the air was bleary. People looked like water drops. The asphalt leaked away from itself.

The light turned, and I crossed the street on the diagonal. JB's Automotive, the auto shop where Nick worked summers, was the nicest one of the corner three, with a white, blue, and green striped outside and a brand-new painted inside. You had to walk past the pumps to get to the repair shop, and I did, weaving between two fueling-up SUVs and over the hump of the island and in through the wide-open doors of the shop, where a shiny red Ford Focus was suspended above the concrete floor, like a ladybug on someone's finger. On the long back wall a row of tools and cans sat arranged, it seemed to me, by size and color, and there was a steel table piled high with catalog stacks and tubes and things, and above the desk there was a bunch of hooks and dangling sets of keys. The place sounded like air being sucked in and cranked out and wheezing. I called for Nick. From out behind the Focus his dad appeared. He was short and muscular with tree-trunk arms. He had a movie-star mustache and thick graying hair, a *JB* sewn onto his uniform pocket. He took his time remembering.

"Rosie?" he asked after a while. "Rosie Keith?"

"Nick's friend," I said. I shifted in my tennis shoes. Pulled a loose strand of hair behind one ear. "From next door."

"All coming back to me," he said, tapping

one side of his head with a blackened index finger. Then he said: "Just kidding with you, Rosie. I didn't forget."

"Nick around?" I asked.

"Placing parts orders in the back office," he said. "You want him?"

I felt my face turn red.

"Hold on."

I stayed put. Watched Nick's dad disappear into a back room, watched Nick come out behind him a few minutes later. He was so much like his dad, only taller: the same wide arms, the same thick hair, the same gray-blue cotton shirt with the *JB* sewn onto the pocket, the way of standing there, looking me over, a slow smile crawling up his face.

"Hey," he said, in the sleepy voice that makes teachers think he's not listening.

"Hey," I answered. He put his big arms out to hug me. I hugged his bigness back.

"What's up?"

I shrugged. "You busy?"

Nick looked at his dad, who also shrugged. Nick heaved his shoulders. "Just the Focus," he said, looking at me, then turning toward his dad. "Until eleven o'clock, when a Wrangler's coming in. Right, boss?"

Nick's dad flicked one big-thumbed, greasy hand toward the town's center. "Just be back," he said, "for the Wrangler."

We walked out of the shade of the shop into the heat of the day, which had sunk down even lower. The commuter traffic was gone, and in its place were all the midmorning moms. "You hear about Rocco?" Nick said when the light turned green.

"What about Rocco?"

"Parents sent him to some college prep boot camp. Can you picture it?"

"No," I said, thinking of Rocco's square face and crooked class-clown smile. "I can't, actually. He's probably stolen everybody's socks by now."

"Probably."

"Probably tried to flirt with one of the teachers."

"That would be Rocco."

We had crossed over to the other side. Mr. D'Imperio was down the street a ways, putting up some ribbon of a sign, and there was a burst of balloons tied to Whiz Bang's glass front door. Three of the bleached mannequins from the everything store had been dragged outside and dressed with ancient bathing suits, to advertise some summer sale of garden tools and beach rafts. I walked so that a part of me was tucked inside Nick's shadow. "How's the auto-repair business?" I asked.

"Same."

"Anything good about it?"

"You're funny, Rosie. Real funny."

"You like Sweet Loaves cinnamon buns?"

"Haven't had one for forever."

"Weird," I said.

We'd gotten as far as Sweet Loaves, and I pulled open the door. Nick stood behind me, held it. "Well, if it isn't Miss Keith," said Jimmy Vee, the proprietor's son. He was twenty-three, tall and sweet, with that blond-brown hair color that doesn't go by much of a name, and he had raisin eyes that squinted to tiny when he smiled. Jimmy Vee worked for his dad in the summer. The rest of the time he was getting his Ph.D. He had graduated number one from Somers High, and his picture had hung in the valedictorian display case ever since, the teachers still speaking of him as if he belonged to them, as if they had made him who he was. "One?" he said. "Or two?" He gestured toward the wedge of glass case that was devoted to buns.

"Two for now," I told him. "One to go."

"You expanding your repertoire?" Jimmy asked me, bending down to half his size to pull a tray of buns from the case. I didn't know how he could stand it, working summers alongside such sweets. I'd have had to eat three buns a day at least. I'd have had raisins for ears and a snout.

"You know Nick?" I asked.

"Seen him around," Jimmy said. The two nodded at each other over the counter.

"JB's Automotive," Nick said, as if that explained him.

"Rosie here is one of our VIP customers," Jimmy said, speaking directly to Nick now, as if I weren't even there. He put two of the buns on plates, lowered the other into a crisp white bag.

"She's something else," Nick said, and I felt my face blush. Dug into my pockets for cash.

"My treat," Nick said.

"Nope," I said. "I invited. I insist."

"Get her next time," Jimmy said, taking my dollar bills and my change.

My face was a furnace getting hotter and hotter. I grabbed our stuff and moved it to one of the round tables with the ice-cream parlor chairs. Nick sat down across from me. I smiled stupidly. He reached for his plate.

"You eat these with your hands?" he said.

"Leave nothing behind," I said.

We sat for a while eating, not talking. We watched some customers come and go, moms buying bread for their families, dads buying doughnuts for themselves, one funny-looking man with too-long hair in a Hawaiian shirt requesting a custom cake for later that week. "Vanilla," he kept saying, "with pink doodad flowers. A girl's cake. Real sweet. That's what I want." When it got too busy, Jimmy's dad would push through the silver doors that divided the customers from the bake shop. He was as wide as Jimmy was tall. Jimmy, we all thought, had been adopted.

"Nick?" I finally said.

"Yeah?"

"I kind of have a question."

He lifted his broad shoulders, let them fall back down. He looked at me, straight on, eyes in my eyes. It was like a fishhook dropping down my throat and snagging my gut. It took me a second or two to remember what it was I'd meant to say.

"My granddad"—finally I got it out—"is dying."

"Oh," Nick said. His eyes hooked even deeper into mine. It felt as if I'd fallen straight through sky.

"And my mom—"

"I know." He stopped me to save me from having to say. "I've seen her." He looked at me, looked at me so hard I heard myself swallow, fishhook in the gut and all, nerves from toes to ears.

"Remember the girl from the train?" I said.

He thought a second: "The performer? With the barrettes?"

I nodded. "Remember you dancing?"

"I wasn't dancing." He looked away from me, out through the glass door, to the street, which had quieted down now that the trains had gone off peak. He turned to look at the counter where Jimmy Vee was standing, but if

Jimmy had heard me talking dance, he didn't let on. He was using glass cleaner on the counter and cases, making room for the bread.

"Your feet were," I said, soft as I could.

"Maybe," he said. "Maybe."

"Your feet were good."

"I wasn't watching my feet."

"I was." I knew I was trespassing deep into the danger zone. I kept trespassing. "I'm dancing now, Nick. I'm—" I sort of turned in my chair and made a gesture toward the vicinity of the House of Dance.

"Well, that's cool," he said, but I could tell he was confused. I could tell he was mostly worrying about what this had to do with him.

"Yeah. Well, I'm kind of having a party."

He looked at me, quizzical. He pushed back against the ice-cream parlor chair. Crossed his arms over his chest and his JB's Automotive logo, let his eyebrows drop low, and waited, while I sat pinned to my seat, hunting for words.

"My granddad," I said again, "is dying."

"I know," he said. "You told me."

"Dancing is the opposite of dying," I said.

He looked at me strangely, a look of wonder on his face. A look that said, "Come on, Rosie. Say it."

"Dancing is going somewhere without packing your bags. Like you did on the train when the girl sang. Dancing is the thing I'm giving Granddad."

"You're a good soul," Nick said, after a very long time.

"I want you to come to a party," I said. "A dance party, right down the street. At my granddad's house."

"I'll come," he said.

I leaned across the table then and gave him a big kiss. "There's something I want you to see," I said. "Can you meet me at Granddad's tomorrow?"

TWENTY-SEVEN

I DIDN'T GET TO GRANDDAD'S HOUSE until noon that day, and when I got there, he was sleeping. Teresa was sitting nearby, with one of his faded magazines open in her hands. She looked up when I walked in. Smiled at me, sadly.

"How is he?" I asked

"Something over the weather," she said, chewing her lip a little.

"Under," I said, my heart falling right down into the cave of my chest. "Under the weather." Granddad had a T-shirt on, soft cotton pants with a drawstring belt. There was a little white box of eyedropper-shaped tubes nearby, and beside the tubes a bowl of what seemed like red sponge lollipops. Tanks like those that astronauts wore were propped up on the floor. A thin plastic line of oxygen snaked up and settled in his nose. Another line snaked from somewhere else and down into a plastic bag.

"He's comfortable," she said. "Sleeping."

I shook my head to fight back tears.

"Last night was a hard night," she said.

"But there's still time? You said there was time?"

"Of course."

I sat down on the hard-as-a-pan wheelchair, and out from between the tanks of oxygen Riot appeared. Nudged her face against the wheelchair wheel, then jumped up onto my lap, one pretty arching leap, nearly crushing the Sweet Loaves bag that I'd been carrying around in the July sun since leaving Nick a little while before. "For you," I said, leaning past the cat and toward Teresa, surrendering the bag. I smacked a few hot tears off my cheeks, then settled back and put one hand on Riot. The cat pressed her front paws into my lap and mewed. Tried to touch her nose to mine. I bent toward her.

"Well, Rosie," Teresa said, "how about that?" She opened the bag, releasing the cinnamon smell. "Nothing like this," she said, "where I come from." She tore off a piece of bun to taste. She licked her sticky fingers.

"What do we do now?" I asked, and she knew what I meant.

"What we can," she said.

"Take care?"

"Take care."

My grandfather looked smaller than ever inside the silver-railed bed, and the room seemed wider and longer than just a month before, when it was the two of us and the cat and the newspaper towers and the brown-cow couch and the coffee cups and the magazines and the jammed-up things on things. Stripped down that way, I could know at last how my granddad and grandmother might have seen the house when they were young, a couple in love, not parents yet, no places not gone, no dances not danced.

"I never got around to cleaning out Granddad's closet," I confessed to Teresa.

"He's fast asleep," she said. "You wouldn't be disturbing."

"You think?" I said.

"A promise is a promise," she said.

I put my hands under Riot's big belly and, as gently as I could, lifted her up, then over onto Teresa's lap. The cat did a quick rub of a cheek with a paw, walked a tight circle, then went back down to sleep. I pushed myself out of the wheelchair and crossed the room to the heavy paneled closet doors, put my hands on the brass knobs, and pulled.

Every square inch inside was jammed

with shelves. Every shelf was jammed with things. A box of rusted garden tools. A sleeve of nails and hooks. A bag of lipstick tubes. Sweaters with tags. Sweaters without tags. Boxes of Kleenex. Rolls of snowman wrapping paper, rolls of angel wrapping paper, a bag of golden ribbons, a crushed red bow, an off-color roll of Scotch tape. There was a can of mosquito spray, and some bottles of lotion. Two bags of crushed birdseed. A carton of lightbulbs. Stacks of orange paper cups. A pair of brown shoelaces. A box of envelopes and a roll of stamps and some staples, pink erasers, boxes I couldn't see into, stuffed-fat brown paper bags, more newspapers, more magazines all tied together with string. It all seemed bigger than a King Tut dig. I stood staring—high and wide.

"There's some Hefty," I heard Teresa say behind me, "in the kitchen."

But I didn't turn, and I didn't answer, and I didn't know what to feel at first, because down on the closet floor, set aside from all the rest, the sun beaming it bright with a spotlight, was a miniature wicker basket, like a cradle, and inside that cradle a fabric doll tucked deep and safe. The doll had blue button eyes and dark yarn hair, and she was staring up at me, her little pink-thread mouth all caught up in a bow, or in a rose, her mouth like a rose. She wore a faded yellow dress with a lacy petticoat. Her fabric feet were bare. She was old and worn but new to me, and I scooped her into my arms.

"Rosie." I heard my name behind me now, my granddad's voice, a sleepy whisper.

I turned. He was facing in my direction, his eyes halfway open, his legs loose in the bed.

"Your mother's favorite doll," he said, his voice small.

I stepped toward him, gently cradling the doll. "This doll was named Rosie?" I asked, perplexed.

"That doll's your namesake," Granddad

234

said. "Made for your mom by your grand-mother even before your mom was born." I was standing at his bedside now, on the not-sick side of the silver railing. His face seemed paper-thin in places, shone straight through by the sun. His words had a different way about them. There were stretches of silence between sounds.

"She knew she was having a girl?"

"She was sure."

"She made this doll?"

"Sewed up every inch."

"And Mom?"

"She loved that doll more than anything. And then she grew up. And then she had you." He closed his eyes when he was saying that, began fanning one hand in front of his face, as if the sun were a creature with wings and he could chase it past him.

"I'm cleaning out your closet, Granddad," I said, and now there were tears I couldn't fight on my face.

"You're one brave girl."

"I think there's going to be a ton of In Trusts," I said, sniffing.

"You're in charge, Rosie Keith. You know best."

"I'm thinking more is better than less."

"I like the way you think."

"Mr. D. says I'm a chip off the old block."

"Better than this block," he said.

"Nope. As fine as. Through and through."

"I got lucky three times in life," he said. "Your grandmother. Your mother. And then you."

TWENTY-EIGHT

NICK MET ME AT MY GRANDDAD'S back step, just as we had planned, and we walked without talking for a while, because I couldn't talk, couldn't say the things that I was thinking. I had finished cleaning Granddad's closets, and I knew what that meant. I had made a party, and the party was soon, and after that would be the thing that no one anywhere could stop from happening. Nick was on the sunny side, and he kept me in shade, and when the sidewalk got crowded, he walked just slightly ahead, steering the people off, it seemed to me, for the sake of my protection. I had invitations to the party in my bag, and whenever we got to the door of an invitee, I'd slip a note through the mail slot. Nick didn't ask me about my day. He understood; we understood each other.

At the House of Dance Nick followed me, through the street door, up the long steps, through the door to the studio lobby. "You can't be shy here," I told him, "because at the House of Dance they will not let you." And right like that, at that very instant, Nick and I and our quiet mood were all rearranged by dancers. Eleanor had taken it on herself to chuck Nick under the chin and Annette was laughing and Marissa was saying, "Will you give them room?" but it was Max who got things in order.

"Aren't we here for some sort of rehearsal?" he asked, and everyone nodded, and Nick looked at me, and I looked back at him, but I said nothing. "I want one run-through of every single dance, and then we will put them in order," Max said. Julia was wearing her best purple shoes. Peter wore a shirt that was the greatest goldfinch color. Teenie had come all dressed up in the brightest splash of pink.

"I'll go get Nick his seat," I said, for I was getting nervous, and this was almost it, and I hooked my arm into his, and the dancers moved to either side so that Nick and I could pass through. His boots made funny sounds on the wood floor. We walked all the way to the wall of windows. "Best seat in the House," I said, pointing at the sill. But he didn't even see the sill; he saw the town that we'd grown up in.

"Bird's-eye view," he said, his eyes wide and sky blue.

And I said, "I knew you'd like it."

"Higher than my roof."

"It is."

"Better perspective."

And I watched him look in all directions—up at sky, down at the town, across at the birds and at the people—while behind him Max took up his post in the music booth and the dancers formed a line, and while beside Nick I felt my stomach clench into a painful knot.

"My granddad's dying," I said.

"I know," Nick said.

"I only have one chance to make his party right."

"Maybe," Nick said. "But I'm betting on you." And then he faced my way and kissed me. Held me as if it didn't matter that all the world could see.

TWENTY-NINE

ONCE WHEN I WAS five-getting-close-to-six, my celebrity dad, my mom, and I went to the shore for a whole seven-day week. We all got new bathing suits, and I got new buckets, and there was a chocolate-brown raft with a pair of yellow strings that we rode, the three of us, as if we were riding a horse straight across the white-fenced sea. We were the Keiths, and we were something. My dad dug the deepest hole of all the sand holes, deep enough for me to stand in. He tossed torn-up bread bits to the gulls to get them speaking English. He talked the lifeguards into letting me sit up high, where they sat, so that I could get a glimpse of the horizon. We ate ice cream every night—two scoops a cone, ordering by way of colors instead of flavors. "A white and a purple for the little miss," my dad would say. "A pastel pink and a touch of springtime yellow for my very beautiful wife. Please." He gave the ice-cream girls five-dollar tips. They knew our names in no time.

On the second-to-last night we all got dressed in our vacation best—a pink sundress for me, a white one for Mom, a lime-green shirt with yellow stripes for my dad. "Board-walk time," Dad said. We all piled into Dad's blazing red convertible, Mom and Dad in the front and I in the back, leaning so close over Mom's bronzed shoulder that her black hair tangled up with mine. I must have asked a thousand different times if we were there yet. "Are we there?" The moon was pale in the dusk sky. There was a salty ocean breeze.

After a while there was a splatter of white and red lights in the distance. "When we get there"—my father pointed—"we'll be there."

When we got there, I discovered some kind of circus by the sea. I could see helicopters being lifted on big crane arms. Roller coasters screaming through space. Carousels and rocket ships and the dizzy spin of color. We parked in a gravel lot and climbed out of the car, and I took both my parents' hands. I stayed sandwiched between them as we hurried up into the sweet and salty smells, the crowds. There were haunted houses and bright fudge shops and counters full of bleached starfish on one side of the boardwalk, and there was the ocean on the other, and there was the prettiest sound I'd ever heard, the sound of bike wheels spinning fast over the walk's worn planks. I'd never seen anything like it before. I felt famous in a famous place. The dusk had become night; the moon was bright.

"The first thing you do at a boardwalk," my dad told me, after we'd gone past bumper cars and miniature golf grounds and taffy shops, through clumps of friends and lovers and families and kids in swerve races on bikes, "is take a spin on the giant Ferris wheel." He seemed to know where to go—how far down the planks the Ferris wheel was, where to stand in line for tickets, where to stand in line for the ride—and my mom said that a first Ferris wheel ride was so exciting and important that it was best if she watched from down below. "So that I can cheer for you," she said, giving me a kiss on my forehead, and even though I remember feeling scared, I acted brave, holding my father's hand and joining the very long line and waiting without fussing for our turn while the big wheel went around with all its screaming passengers. Finally we were first in line when the big wheel stopped, and on we climbed: I in my pink sundress, my dad in his lime and yellow shirt. A man wearing

244

a red suit and a backward-pointing cap closed us in behind a rusted metal bar.

Then chair by chair we rose, up a very wide curve, stopping at every interval until all the new customers were on board. I could see my mom easily at first, and then she started to grow small, and with every lift upward I felt the breeze grow stronger. Then Dad and I in our chair were at the very highest point, tipping back and forth, as if we were just about to fall. The knuckles of my hands were white. I had that get-sick feeling in my gut. I begged my dad to let me off. "Rosie, don't be silly," he said. "The fun's about to start."

Right after that, as if he had magic powers, the last customer climbed on board, and we were whipping down around the very wide curve, then rising up and up, toward the moon. It felt as if my chin had fallen down around my toes, as if my stomach were all liquid. I was screaming, but everyone was screaming, and my dad said—yelled it loud, so I could hear him—"See that, Rosie. We're having an adventure." He put his arm around me, and I pressed up against him close and never for a second took my hands off the bars, and then, slam, when we were one metal chair away from the wheel's highest spot, the whole thing stopped its turning with a jolt. I thought at first that some lucky kid was climbing off, another customer climbing on. But then nothing happened, and we stayed stuck, and the moon was close and the salt breeze blew, and the sound of everybody's screaming changed from funny into scared. "Dad?" I said. "Dad?" But even he couldn't make the big wheel move.

I knew for sure that we were going to fall, going to smash against the ground like bugs getting smashed against a windshield. "We're going to fall, we're going to fall," I told my dad, but he said, "Technical glitch, Rosie. No problem. Happens all the time." He kept his one arm around me steady, and with his free hand he pointed to the ground where my mother stood, her white sundress all lit up by boardwalk lights. Her eyes were on nothing but us. She didn't move one inch. She was standing there, steadfast. And my dad said, "Nothing's going to happen, see? Your mom wouldn't let us fall." Soon the wheel was going again. Soon I was back down on the ground.

That night when I got home from Granddad's, Mom was there and Mr. Paul wasn't, and something was wrong, it was clear. She was sitting in the living room with the lights turned off, as if I were hours late for a dinner she'd promised, as if she'd been a real mother all summer long. "Mom?" I said when I found her sitting there in the street-lamp dark, when I realized she was alone.

"Rosie?" she said.

"Mom?"

"I'm leaving Mr. Paul," she said. And despite the knot that was my heart, I sat down then to listen.

THIRTY

SOMETIMES YOU KNOW something's wrong, and you tell yourself you'll never do that wrong, and then it happens: You take the first wrong step and then the next, and you're all of a sudden guilty of everything you never thought you could be guilty of. Nothing that you ever do will erase the thing you've done, and since you can't turn back, you don't turn back; you just keep doing wrong. "It was too easy," my mother said that night. "He made it easy. He was there when no one else was."

We kept the lights off in the living room. I sat across from her in the rocking chair she had bought when she learned she was pregnant with me. She stayed where she had been, tucked into the corner of the beat-up couch beside the hutch of curious things. She had opened the windows; a single firefly had flown in. Turned itself on and off between us as Mom talked and I tried to listen. The TV volume was up loud at the Burkemans' next door. There was the usual number of cars for that hour, spilling headlight juice into the room and then trailing off. When the cars went by, I could see my mother's face. When they drove on past, they drained her eyes.

She said that at first Mr. Paul made her feel safe. "Like I had a purpose," she said. She explained that it had felt like an adventure early on, going in and out of people's houses, making things clean, revising the perspective. It was like a Mr. Marinari project, the way she told it—taking in each window-cleaning customer's view, getting a feel for the way the world closed in on other people, the way it opened out. "We had so much to talk about." My mother sighed. "We shared so many secrets. Nobody knew all the things that we knew about the lives of perfect strangers." She was struggling to put her facts in order. "When you're window washing, you're working side by side," she said. "Or you're working face-to-face, across the same pane of glass. You're this close, Rosie," she said, and if I couldn't see her hands just then, I could imagine, sure enough, that they were kissing-inches apart.

"It just all seemed so . . . *inevitable*," she went on, shaking her head slowly as a spill of headlight yellow flooded the room. "Like there was nothing anyone could do. Soul mates, Rosie. Do you know what I mean?" I didn't answer; she wasn't really asking. I was watching the firefly go from dark to light to dark, its light more neon green than yellow, as if it were powered by a battery pack.

"I thought he didn't love her," she said.

"Love who?" I asked, though I knew full well, because the meanest part of me wanted her to have to say it.

"He promised he didn't love her."

The firefly sailed to the farthest corner of the room and stuck. Went on and off like a lantern hanging there in a storm.

"He said he'd marry me. Said he'd change the business name. Call it Mr. and Mrs. Paul."

The firefly lit yellow-green again, and then its light went silent. *Come on, firefly,* I thought. *Come on. Give us some light.* I wasn't looking at my mother, for if I did, I'd know for sure that she was crying.

"He isn't going to." She sighed. "He never was. He loves his wife. He always did; every minute the guy still loved his wife."

"Mr. Paul is a crud head," I said. Because she'd stopped talking and because he was.

"*Ro*sie."

"Plus he's bald."

There was the light of the firefly again, nudging the ceiling, hunting for sky. I watched that thing. I waited. I tried to imagine what she might say next, and then I realized that she was laughing. A broken, wheezing, miserable laugh, as if laughing for her had become a foreign language. As if her lungs didn't work.

"You're funny, Rosie," she said at last.

"Well, he is," I said. The firefly had gone dark again. Something fake hysterical was going down on the Burkemans' TV. I tilted my weight in the rocking chair and rode it back and forth. "You ever look at him?"

"Did I ever look at Mr. Paul?" she said, her voice still crackling, incredulous, dry and wet at the same time, old as the world is old and also squeaking new.

"Did you ever *see* him, I meant. There's a difference."

"How'd you get so smart?" she asked, after a long stretch of silence.

"Mr. Marinari," I said. "School project."

The rocking chair creaked. A car went by. Another burst of canned ha-has let loose from the sitcom next door, and I thought of Nick upstairs in that house with his earphones on, trying not to hear the noise below. I got a glimpse of my mother, her eyes wet and wide, her neck pale and bony, her hands up in her hair. The skin was smudged beneath her eyes. She had no lipstick on. She was forgiven, maybe, or not forgiven, but either way, she was just as pretty as she had ever been. Either way, and I couldn't help it, I would always love my mom.

"What are you going to do now?" I asked.

"Now?" She sniffed.

"Without the bald one."

"Oh, God," she said. "Start over. I guess. Find a better way to be necessary." The firefly I'd thought was gone was hanging now, as if on a string, right above her narrow shoulder. She couldn't see it, but I could. A beacon, Mr. Marinari would have called it. I called it, to myself, a sign.

"I can think of lots of ways," I said.

"What kind of ways?"

"At Granddad's, for example. There's stuff to do."

Her silence.

"He's a bit under the weather," I pressed.

"Worse than before," she said. She knew.

"Getting so. He sleeps in a bed with railings. There are machines."

"Oh. Rosie."

"You're his daughter," I said.

"I've been lousy," she said. "In every direction. Do you think he'd want to see me still? Does he ever talk about me?"

"You should ask him," I said. "Yourself."

She thought a long time, two passing cars' worth, enough time for the firefly to whoosh off and vanish. "What do you do when you're there all day?" she finally wanted to know.

"I sit around. I talk to Teresa. I put his things In Trust."

"In trust?"

"It's a category."

"Oh."

"It's his story."

"I see."

"It's who Granddad is. What he's loved. His choices."

"Sounds like some sort of expedition."

"Sort of. Like today," I said, "I found a doll. He said it was the original Rosie. He told me things. I listened." Suddenly the noise from the TV at the Burkemans' snapped off, making a truer kind of nighttime silence, deepening the darkness. Suddenly the vanished firefly was back, so close I could have taken its glow in my hand and held it there while I weighed what I might tell.

What questions I might ask.

What ways there are of starting over.

"I'm throwing a party for Granddad," I finally said. "And I could use some help."

THIRTY-ONE

WHEN YOU HAUL AWAY THE CLUTTER that cannot matter anymore, you change the size and shape of things, the possibilities. I made decisions on the D.L. I tossed away all the Toss. I bought special boxes at the everything store for all that was In Trust: the travel books, the floating feather, the best-loved novels, the decks of photographs I'd someday spend long hours steaming apart, the parts of the dresses my granddad had set aside to remind him of Aideen. I slipped in the letters and the postcards, the stash of coins and recipe cards, the original Rosie, a sweater my granddad had said he'd worn on the day that I was born. I tucked in every bit of black, round vinyl, every faded record cover, all the parts of the Sansui. My mother came in her old gray Volvo to help me take things home, parked at the curb and put her blinkers on while Teresa and I stacked the boxes into the trunk, then into the long backseat, finally on the floor of the passenger's side, and I didn't even try to hide my tears, and Teresa said it was okay that I was crying. Mom too. Then Mom came back, and she walked through the door of the house she'd long called home, calling for her father. She went to sit with Granddad then, while I dried my face and took the last steps for what would happen next. She sat, and they talked a very long time, beyond and past regrets.

Pastrami's was doing sandwiches on the house, and Mr. D'Imperio himself was coming for the show, bringing his entire corporation along, bringing a vat of fruited ice. Whiz Bang was bouqueting balloons in gleamed-up colors. Jimmy Vee and his dad were doing up a cake; "Sweet Dreams," the icing said. And Annie Pearl in the end brought down the house with any flower that blooms in ruby red, because ruby red is the color of July, which is the color of passion, which is the color of a life being lived. Ruby red is the heart, and ruby red was the color of my borrowed shoes, the color of the dress that Miss Marie had sewn for me. Ruby red bloomed everywhere. It was July 31.

They closed the House of Dance that night; there was no light in those wide window frames. They came down the street, my friends the dancers did, walking the dancer's walk, carrying their clothes before them in plastic bags, their pouches of makeup, their suede-soled dancing shoes. Max was there, of course, and Marissa too, and Annette and

Eleanor and Peter and Teenie and Julia and also William, Marissa's William, who had come in from New York. Nick was already at the house when the dancers arrived, had taken off from JB's like a boyfriend would, to help Teresa set up for the show. They'd moved Granddad's bed and machines against one wall. They'd steered the wheelchair with the tasseled cushion out front and center. They'd put a chair for Mom beside the wheelchair for Granddad, and Granddad was ready; Teresa had made sure. His hair was that much longer than when the summer had started and more gloriously white than before. His ears were large and his eyes were blue, and he didn't have to say that he loved me, not one time, because I absolutely knew.

Upstairs, meanwhile, the air was electric. The second room to the left, the largest room, had been transformed, by my mom, into a dressing area, with three rectangular mirrors propped against one wall and a little folding screen separating the women from the men. It was fishnet hose and silken bathrobes, on the women's side, Danskins and sweats, tubes of vermilion, carmine, emerald, cobalt, cerulean, pink; cheeky crayons and skinny pencils and blushes and clips. It was color, brilliant color, from every corner of the world. Strands of stray ribbon snaked across the floor, fugitive rhinestones. Annette was buffing her shoes.

But it was Marissa I couldn't stop looking at, her candy-red hair in a magnificent sheen, her lashes long and extravagant, her eyes made tropical by all the paints that she'd put on. She held one hand beneath Julia's chin and with her free hand worked that canvas, making the girl glorious, bold. When she had done her work there, she called for me, stretched two long, graceful hands toward my hair to sweep it from my face.

"Some of it loose," she said. "Some of it pinned up. Yes? Something pretty here?" She pressed a rhinestone barrette to a place above my ear, then walked me to the mirrors my mom had bought that very afternoon at the everything store, because she was helping, because she knew. "Beauty, yes? You see it? Yes?"

"I see you beside me," I said.

She kissed me on the cheek; I kissed her, too. I wound my way back down Granddad's steps, toward the room in which we'd spent our summer, the room that had been stripped down to make way, at last, for an adventure. In the front hall, in the darkness, some of the dancers had gathered to rehearse. Ghostly, ethereal, they spooled in and out, tracing the rumba of Cuba, the samba of Brazil, the tango of Argentine cowboys, holding themselves open to invisible hands, preparing to take my grandfather to the places he might have gone, the places he'd been dreaming of, in honor of Aideen. But for the whisk of shoes across the floor there was no sound.

But for a beckoning stomp, a slow skimming of feet, there was nothing but the waiting to begin. What light there was fell from the moon outside, bright and high, touching close to heaven.

There were fifteen minutes until the show began. There were ten. I stepped from the hall back into the kitchen, where Pastrami's sandwiches were on metal trays, where the fruited ice basked in a cooler. I peeked out into the living room, where my granddad sat, with my mom beside him, with Teresa and Mr. D. and Harvey all close, with Miss Marie and Annie Pearl and Jimmy Vee right there too, with Riot in her basket, perfectly preened, with Nick as near as Nick had to be, as he would be all the rest of that summer. The bouquets of balloons were sandbagged to the floor. The flowers were in vases everywhere. There were five minutes until the show was scheduled to begin, and then there were two, and then Max was floating down the stairs, his black hair shellacked, his black shoes on, his hand reaching out for mine.

"Are you ready?" he asked me.

I nodded. "I am."

"Step forward then," he said. "And let it happen."

ACKNOWLEDGMENTS

This time I begin with my husband, Bill, who surprised me one birthday with the gift of dance—ten shared ballroom lessons that endeared us both to the rise and fall, the quick-quick, the learning to lead and to follow. At the immaculate Dancesport Academy in Ardmore, ten lessons became so many more and our teachers became our friends—Scott Lazarov, Stephanie Risser, Aideen O'Malley, John Vilardo, John Larson, Jean Paulovich, and Josephina Luczak. I am amazed by you all, I am grateful for what you've shared. Thank you.

HarperCollins continues to be the most extraordinary, most intelligent, most welcome and welcoming home. Laura Geringer, Jill Santopolo, Lindsey Alexander: You are rare in your commitment to the finest-wrought tales, in your kindness to authors, and in your vision. I am so lucky to have found you. Thank you to the copyeditors, Renée Cafiero and Pearl

Hanig. Thank you to Carla Weise for the art. Thank you to Cindy Tamasi and Nettie Hartsock for spreading the word. Thank you to Jennie Nash for the tube of red lipstick. Thank you to Yvonne Marceau for the seeds.

Amy Rennert, my agent: Well. Who'd have thought it, all those years ago? Who'd have imagined that we'd be here? You are a cherished friend.

House of Dance was written during a time of tremendous personal loss. I miss my mother more than I can say; I wish that she were here, to read this story. I am awed by my father, who carries forward gracefully, planting gardens and taking care. I see, in goldfinch and hawk, how the soul lives on. Finally, as always and of course, I am grateful to my son, Jeremy, who finds the perfect words, who is wise beyond his years, and who has given me song in times of stillness, a surge of joy in moments of seeming emptiness.

Every story is a blessing, and in this life I am so richly blessed